# MATCH WITH THE DEMON

## CHACE VERITY

D1115073

# AUTHOR'S NOTE

Dearest readers,

As I write this note, there are still a few days left in 2021. It's been a hard year. But it's also been a year that has forced me to realize I was never going to be happy if I tried to meet other people's expectations. For a long time, "compromise" was a word etched in my hearts. No one ever saw the real me, not even the people who thought they did. I just wanted to fit in with the people I cared about who didn't seem to care about me. I wanted to be on the "right" path.

But there's no such thing as a "right" path.

Strangely (or perhaps fittingly, if you've read some of my other books), this realization hit me while I was playing a video game. A character's arc woke me up to my reality. Right and wrong is subjective, so I'm gonna have fun.

Maybe not the most optimistic take, but it's how I've been living the last few months of my life—cutting out the people who never supported me, pushing back when people don't respect my boundaries, giving myself sloppy gender-affirming haircuts, laughing on Zoom calls as I talk about the BTS songs I listened to while I wrote gay tentacle sex. My friend circle is much smaller now, but the people who are here now will probably stay with me until our lives' last chapter.

Harrison and Lazlo's journey in *Match with The Demon* echoes these sentiments. They aren't characters who need many people in their lives. Just the folks who really see them. And they have a lot of fun.

I hope you surround yourself with people who accept the real you. If you aren't in a place to do that yet, I hope 2022 is the year where you'll start making steps to living your truest life. I'm cheering for you.

Best,

Chace "is going to continue to write very weird romances and have fun doing it" Verity

# CONTENT NOTES

- Main character estranged from his family because of his sexuality
    - Multiple references to transactional sex
    - Use of nicotine and alcohol
    - Brief references to marijuana
    - Explicit depiction of sex between a human and a demon in chapters ten and twelve with some bondage and light breathplay (yes, the tentacles are involved, you're welcome)

# CHAPTER 1

*H*arrison stared at the message sitting in his MapleMance inbox, ignoring the flurry of power drills and circular saws behind him. There was no way he had matched with someone so ludicrously hot and muscular. There wasn't much information in the man's profile except that he worked for the city. Was he a bot? A scammer? Harrison had heard stories from his straight coworkers of "supermodels" ghosting them on dating apps after receiving some money from them.

But the guy—*Laz*—seemed eager to meet him. Wanted to know if Harrison was available for dinner in a couple of nights. And, Christ, the guy's cheekbones were sharp enough to cut a basement window out of a concrete foundation.

Harrison Hamilton the Happy Handyman was very available. And very nervous.

His divorce had happened more than a decade ago. It had been two decades since he had gone on a date with someone new. And this was his first prospect with the gender he actually liked.

As much as he had cherished his partner and mother of

his wonderful son, he just had never been attracted to women. Tricked himself into thinking he had been for the sake of his close-minded family. Almost succeeded. But, no, he was definitely gay. His ex had deserved someone who could love her the way she wanted. It was dishonest to have half-assed sex with her once a week and dodge all of her attempts to go on romantic dates.

He had left the marriage, prepared to only see his son every other weekend as a form of punishment for lying about his sexuality. His family had treated him like a demon when he came clean to them, so it had been safe to assume his ex would wield his long history of lying against him in court.

But life had had other plans. His ex had found a new man pretty quickly during the divorce proceedings and bolted across Canada to move in with the maritimer. Harrison had been left to raise Justin on his own in the only part of Alberta he'd ever known, where the Bow River promised to outlive the city that wanted to outgrow it.

Laz's gorgeous profile picture stared at Harrison as he contemplated how to respond. He wasn't good with new things, even though he had challenged himself to have a date for Valentine's Day.

"Uh, Hamtaro, what's going on? Thought you were only stepping outside for a quick cigarette."

Harrison shot his coworker, Gary, a glare and shoved his phone in his pocket. "I haven't been gone that long."

Gary shrugged, lighting up a cigarette himself. His safety goggles dangled around his neck—their perpetual home. Of the Happy Handymen crew, Harrison was the only one who always wore his protective gear. The other guys could afford to have some accidents, but he couldn't. Raising an ambitious kid who had wanted to try every sport and join every club at school had been expensive.

Although, that kid wasn't really a kid anymore. Justin was

in his second semester of university, and he had elected to live on campus this semester. The last few weeks had been painfully quiet as Justin didn't share many details about himself over the phone. All that Harrison knew about his son's new life was that he had applied for a job at a hardware store and that he hated getting up at nine o'clock in the morning for classes.

While he was thinking about him, Harrison decided he should call Justin and asked about the job thing again. His son had worked for the Stampede a few times, but he had never held a job that needed him for more than two weeks. Justin seemed excited about making some extra money for school.

Harrison pulled out his phone and gave his kid a ring. No answer. As to be expected. Maybe he was in a class. Or, more realistically, he was sleeping off a hangover. Justin was the epitome of a Canadian party-going teenager.

After hanging up, Harrison found himself looking at MapleMance again. Specifically, at Laz's profile picture. Did someone that attractive with such an elegant nose and a playful smile really want to spend a couple of hours in a restaurant with a single dad going through empty nest syndrome?

"What the fuck?" Gary broke into laughter, which rang loudly in Harrison's ear. The less-than-happy Handyman could feel the sticky, smokey breath rolling down his neck. "You're on a dating site?"

"Shut up." Harrison flipped him the bird, and then he realized he was actually talking to the King of Getting Catfished. "Fine. Since you already saw, yes. This guy wants to go out with me. Do you think he's real?"

Gary grabbed the phone. "I don't know anything about men, and honestly, I don't know why you think anyone would be interested in you based on your profile pic."

Heat swelled through Harrison's cheeks. "What's wrong with my profile pic?"

"It's just you. You combed your hair? And you shaved for it? You've always got some scruff, Blondie. Do gay men not like a bit of ruggedness? Or did you not at least have some summer pics where you have a tan? You're so white and pale here. Should have taken a picture of you covered in sawdust or holding a trout you caught. Something manly."

Was…cleaning up for the profile pic not a good idea? Or maybe taking advice from *Gary*, of all people, was a bad idea.

Harrison snatched his phone back. "So you think I'm getting scammed?"

Gary nodded. "Probably. But who knows? I've gotten laid a bunch through MapleMance with some mega babes."

"Have you…?" Harrison tipped his head to the side, recalling the many, many stories of Gary's dating failures.

"We should get back to work." Gary quickly put out his cigarette in the snow pile next to him. "These windows don't install themselves."

True enough. And their small crew meant that it was only the new kids working inside. They had passion and competence, but they were still prone to mistakes.

While Gary stepped back inside the house, Harrison gave his inbox another look. Laz's picture and sudden dinner invitation promised a mistake, but…

He kind of wanted to make a mistake. He had spent his youth maintaining an image that would keep him safe from his family's bigoted barbs. And his adulthood had been devoted to caring for a child who acted impulsively. For just once in Harrison Hamilton's life, he wanted to be a little careless.

Though he nearly choked on his heart while he typed the message, he sent the very handsome Laz a response.

*I'm free to meet up with you.*

# CHAPTER 2

*I*t had been quite a relief when Laz had suggested a sports bar as a place to grab food. Harrison didn't own a lot of nice clothes, so a sports bar date meant that he could get away with a decent flannel henley and some new-ish jeans under his winter coat. And if the conversation was too awkward, they could watch hockey or play billiards.

Still, when Valentine's Day and the agreed upon dinnertime rolled around, Harrison found it difficult to get out of his truck. The comforting heater and the rumble of his engine running were familiar. Whatever was inside was not. Sure, he had been to sports bars over the years with friends, but this was *different*. He was a thirty-nine-year-old gay man going on his first date with another man.

Something tasted like rust in the back of his throat as he grew more apprehensive. He could always taste metal when he was worried. Often, it was his tongue that would first let him know when he was on the precipice of a nerve-induced storm.

What if Laz didn't show up? Worse, what if he did show up, and they had a terrible time together? Or—the worst possible case scenario—what if Harrison fell hardcore in love with Laz at first sight and Laz realized he was, in fact, far too handsome for someone who had a subscription to *Popular Mechanics*?

A full body shudder rolled through Harrison. Was it too late to cancel? He hadn't actually told anyone about the date, not after Gary shared his suspicions. Nobody at work would harass him, and Justin probably had no interest in his dad's dating life.

Well. That wasn't true. Justin had suggested online dating in the first place. But that had been while they were unloading the teenager's belongings from the truck, and a very lovely young lady in a tight sweater dress had walked by. It was obvious Justin didn't want his dad to call him three times a day and cramp his style.

Harrison snorted. Did people even say *you're cramping my style* these days? Ah, that would be a good question to ponder while he got miserably drunk at home later with his hamsters and the best of Nickelback.

The date was going to be a disaster. That much was clear. But he had told someone over MapleMance that he would be here for Valentine's Day. So he had to show up.

*Might as well get it over with.*

Harrison trudged into the sports bar and took his time kicking the snow off his boots at the door. The telltale hubbub of hockey games blared in one corner of the building. If tonight was humiliating, at least he could drown in yelling at referees with the fans decked in red.

Flashy lights from the arcade games by the main bar caught his eye. One game machine had some kind of kraken attached to the back—that would be interesting to investigate later.

The other side of the bar had billiard tables, all empty. Most of the action seemed to be around the TVs. There were mostly men there, none of whom looked like they should be a 6'4" chiseled Greek god.

Catfished. Great.

*Okay, maybe he's just late.*

Harrison removed his gloves and sent Laz a message through the dating app. *I'm here.*

No sooner had he taken two steps inside did he receive a reply. *Me too! I got us a table at the high tops.*

High tops? Harrison glanced around, but he didn't see any tall tables. Was he at the wrong bar?

Another message from Laz arrived. *They're on the other side of the arcade games.*

Ah. Harrison swallowed hard as he slowly crossed the bar. His heart pounded in his ears, and his throat throbbed with anticipation. *Someone* was here to meet him.

Someone was going on a date with the Happy Handyman. Someone possibly very hot.

Harrison finally arrived at the sea of high tops. Only one table had a pitcher of beer with empty glasses beside them and a bottle of hand sanitizer. That must have been Laz's table, but...

Where was the MapleMance Adonis? In the bathroom? Watching the hockey game?

As Harrison took a seat—pausing to set his gloves and coat on another stool—he found himself drawn to the arcade games. Particularly, his attention was centered on the one with the kraken.

Now that he had a view of the back, he didn't understand what he was looking at. The crimson tentacles moved, but they were attached to a short mannequin's sides. The creature didn't seem to be a part of a game.

Then the creature waved at him. With both its hand and a tentacle.

7

Harrison jumped, nearly falling off his stool. Was it an animatronic? Why would the bar have something so weird?

As the animatronic started approaching him, everything became way more confusing. The tentacles swayed with the mannequin's fluid motions. Well, it must have been a real man. But one with an eerily realistic alien makeup job, including golden eyes that practically glowed. Ruby red jewels were woven in the flame-like hair the strange man had pulled back into a ponytail. More crimson gems were scattered across his pale skin.

And there was a lot of skin showing—the creature wore a vest that only covered his front and back, some ripped sweatpants, and duct taped flip-flops.

"Sorry!" A gravelly voice stumbled out of the thing as it took a seat across from Harrison. "I was checking to see if anyone had lost any good garbage behind the arcade machines. I only found some coins and a lighter. You want it? Your profile says you smoke, right?"

Harrison covered his face, trying to process what was happening.

Not tall. Not buff. Okay, Laz had a thick figure Harrison *did* like, but the profile had suggested a different kind of build.

Harrison looked up again at his Valentine's Day date. Why was Laz not offering an explanation for the costume? Was the handsome guy in the profile pic a social media star playing a prank on a lonely windows installer?

And…did he have really large tentacles for legs instead of feet? Why did the tentacles all move so realistically?!

"Laz?" Harrison kept his voice low. "You're Laz?"

The creature broke into a grin. "Harrison! The Happy Handyman! You're much pinker than your profile picture indicated."

"Because I'm either horrifically embarrassed or about to

be really pissed," Harrison muttered, debating if he should quickly down the pitcher of beer in one go. Make Laz the Comedian pay for it.

"What?" Laz's face contorted into a confused scowl. His ensuing pout revealed some tiny gems embedded along the inside of his pretty mouth. "You got an ex-boyfriend in here or something? Awkward. We can go somewhere else."

Harrison shot him a glare. "You know that's not what I'm talking about, and you have a lot of nerve to sit there, pretending you don't know why I'm mortified."

"I don't know, actually." Laz blinked. "Do I look different from my profile picture? I messed with the filters some—"

"The tentacles!" Harrison hissed, reaching for the pitcher. "My first gay Valentine's Day is with someone who is dressed as a kraken or something."

Laz's jaw dropped open. "Holy shit. You can see them?"

"Of course!" Harrison poured himself a glass of beer.

"Who are you?" Laz's grin returned, this time brighter than before. "How are you able to see the real me?"

*Huh?*

Something about the date had gotten stranger, but Harrison had no way to predict which way the conversation was headed.

"You mind repeating that?" Harrison asked. "You're being quite ridiculous if you think no one can see that costume."

"Ah, is this your first time on a date with a demon?"

Harrison hurriedly guzzled down the beer and immediately poured himself another. He did not, in any form or fashion, want to go along with the gag.

Laz's tentacles tapped the side of the table as he drummed his manicured fingers along his chin. The red gems glued to his black nails sparkled under the amber pendant lights.

"Okay," Laz said. "This is my first time on a date with a human, actually, so we can both be freely awkward now

9

that we know I'm a demon. Wow! This dating app stuff is legit."

"Excuse me, but you can stop the prank now. I'm humiliated enough." Harrison brought the glass to his lips, studying the weirdo in front of him.

All right, if he had to be into people dressed up oddly, he could potentially be into the thing before him. Laz was attractive, despite the makeup, and probably into kinky shit. The guy also had to be massively rich to afford the tentacle attachments.

But why did he dress like he had found his outfit in a dumpster? Surely there would be a fancy robe or something to go with the costume. Was he cosplaying an anime character? Justin had been heavily into cosplay when he was in high school. And LARPing, for a brief spell.

Was that what this Laz was doing? LARPing? The details of his costume were incredible. The undersides of the crimson tentacles had golden suckers that seemed to move independently from the rest of the appendages.

"Okay, so this is your first time talking to a demon." Laz nodded nonchalantly. "Cool. I don't actually know how to convince you that I'm a real demon, but we might as well get on with our date, shouldn't we?"

Maybe the beer had hit Harrison already. Maybe he knew he'd be unable to sleep tonight if he went home without any answers. Maybe he just wanted to follow through with his mistake.

"Fine," he found himself saying. "Let's continue our date."

"Great!"

Laz waved toward the bar until a server made her way to them. She greeted both of them with a bright smile, completely unfazed by the writhing tentacles. Ugh. She must have been in on the prank too.

"Hey, guys, can I get you some more drinks or something

to eat?" The server handed them a menu. "Our Valentine's Day special is our jumbo poutine platter topped with house-made brown gravy, jalapeño slices, and heart-shaped cheese curds. Totally shareable between two people, lovers or not."

*People.* Harrison turned his glare to Laz. The server knew who he was underneath the costume.

"Yeah, bring us one of those." Laz gestured to the pitcher with a tentacle, then he quickly held his hand toward it. "We'll take another one of these too. My date seems to like cheap shit like me. Harrison—can I call you Harrison—what else do you want?"

Harrison scanned the menu, but he found himself unable to read anything. Too many voices swam in his mind. Almost all of them told him to get up and leave.

The only voice that told him to stay couldn't give him an actual reason to stay.

"That's fine for now," Harrison mumbled. "Thanks."

The server took the menu with her and left, promising to be back in a few minutes. Once again, Harrison was alone with his unusual Valentine's Day date. He stared at one of Laz's tentacles as it picked up the pitcher.

Christ, this was not how he had imagined his first date with a man to go.

"Go ahead and ask me anything." Laz poured himself a beer with his tentacle. As the glass filled, he rested his chin on his hands. "You probably have a lot of questions about demons."

It would take a calculator from NASA to add up every-thing bouncing in Harrison's head. But he decided to start with something small. Something that didn't entertain the demon fantasy.

"'Laz' is an unusual name." Harrison watched as a tentacle brought the glass to its owner's mouth. "Short for some-thing? Lazlo?"

"What? No." His date's eyes widened. "But I like that. *Lazlo*. I panicked when I first got here and just made a sound roll out of my mouth. Lazlo. Yeah, that's a good name. I'm gonna start using that. Call me 'Lazlo' from now on. Let me write this down."

In a flash, one of Laz—Lazlo's—tentacles produced his phone for him. His beer-holding tentacle kept feeding him the dark amber beverage while his fingers tapped furiously on his screen.

Harrison took a long drink. "Okay, Lazlo. I guess to answer your earlier question, you can call me Harrison."

"Oh, good. I wasn't sure if that was your actual given name. Harrison. Hamilton. Those are surnames, aren't they?"

"And first names." Harrison cringed. "My parents were fond of alliteration. My sister is Hadley Hamilton. Well, was. She's married now."

*And hasn't spoken to me since I came out.*

Lazlo looked up from his phone. "You mentioned in your MapleMance profile that you're an Aries. And your nickname is 'Hamtaro.' Ooh, more alliteration?"

For some reason, a flush of embarrassment swept through Harrison. Logically, a silly nickname backstory should pale in comparison to the weirdo getup. But...

"Kind of." Harrison took another drink. The back of his neck burned fiercely as he met Lazlo's curious eyes. "I've always had hamsters for pets. Even now, I have a couple of dwarf hamsters for roommates. My coworkers find it, uh, amusing."

"That's awesome. A rodent lover." One of Lazlo's tentacles grabbed the pitcher and brought it toward Harrison's half-empty glass. "Rodents are totally my style. Real shame I chose the one area in the world where there aren't rats. Rat rats. Not politician rats."

The absurdity of the situation finally settled in, allowing

Harrison to chuckle at the quip. Or maybe he was a bit tipsy already. Didn't take much to get him buzzed these days.

"And how did you 'choose' Calgary? Where did you come from?" Harrison started taking another long sip.

Lazlo's eyes danced around the room. "Oh, where don't I come from? You live for a few thousand years as a pleasure demon, you kinna come from everywhere. And come everywhere."

It took everything Harrison had not to spit out his drink. Some of the beverage escaped his mouth, anyway. One of Lazlo's tentacles helpfully grabbed a napkin and wiped his mouth for him. Then it scampered under the table with the used napkin.

"Sorry." Harrison stared at him as the pitcher-bearing tentacle refilled his glass. "A pleasure demon?"

"Yeah, but that's not what I wanna be anymore." Lazlo shrugged. "Gets boring banging horny creatures after a while, you know? I met this judgment demon recently, and he directed me to new forms of pleasure. So now I'm a trash demon."

Oh, yeah. This guy was into kinky shit.

And Harrison was not entirely unsure if he was disinterested.

"What does a trash demon do?" asked the human who truthfully wanted to know more about the pleasure demon business.

"I mentioned on my MapleMance profile that I work for the city, right?" Lazlo fussed with his ponytail and sported a proud curl to his lips. "I do waste management! Humans throw away so much stuff they think is worthless. It's amazing."

Harrison blinked. "You literally meant trash, eh?"

"That's right, eh!" A boisterous laugh tumbled out of Lazlo. "You Canadians talk especially cute. I suppose that's why I wanted to start my new life here. Plus, the snow thing is pretty cool. Sometimes it gets in my shoes and turns into mud. That's wicked."

"I can tell you haven't lived here for very long." Harrison downed most of his beer, eyeing the server approaching with another pitcher and the poutine. "Six to eight months of winter every year for nearly four decades has dispelled the magic of snow for me."

Lazlo ran his tongue along his lower lip, studying Harrison. His red tongue had little jewels on it as well. A hint of something golden on the underside peeked out for a moment.

Had he attached suckers to his tongue as well? Why? Wasn't that uncomfortable?

As the server set down the jumbo platter of poutine and fresh pitcher of beer, Harrison waited for Lazlo to remove the adornments from his mouth. Instead, his date squirted hand sanitizer onto his palms, rubbed his hands as he thanked the server, and dove into the poutine without any silverware once she was gone.

Harrison sanitized his hands as well, keeping his gaze on his unusual date who uttered an appreciative groan when he popped a heart-shaped cheese curd into his mouth. Slowly, Harrison picked up his fork and stacked the cutlery with an excellent balance of gravy-covered fries and toppings.

He chewed on that perfect first bite and decided that, yes, he was on a date with a demon. The tentacles and golden eyes could be rationalized. But there was no way anyone could eat poutine that recklessly if they were at risk for swallowing costume jewels.

It was probably too late to freak out over having a greasy Valentine's Day meal in a sports bar with an actual demon. But it was not too late to be thoroughly confused. How had he matched with a *demon* on his first foray into queer dating? What in the fuck was a demon doing on a dating app?

Well, it was probably okay to ask that question, actually.

"So why did you sign up for a dating app if you were tired of…" Harrison swallowed the rest of his bite. "Banging horny creatures, I believe is how you phrased it?"

"Dating doesn't mean banging, right?" Lazlo winked at him as he stuck a fry in his mouth. "Who knows? Banging might be interesting again after I dig through some trash. And according to the delightful women I work with, there are a lot of trashy men on dating apps."

Harrison gaped at him blankly, his fork hovering over the poutine. "Is that why you messaged me? Did I look trashy?"

There was no way he was *trashy*. That word suited the misogynistic rubbish known as Gary.

Lazlo shook his head. The tips of his tentacles swayed with his motion. "The opposite of that! I heard the more handsome the guy, the more of a piece of shit he is on the inside. And you were the hottest dude over thirty with the 'interested in men' box checked."

That…

Was a compliment, right? Harrison frowned and had another bite of poutine.

Lazlo placed a jalapeño on the tip of his tongue and took his time swallowing it. An observation brimmed in his bright eyes.

"What?" Harrison asked. "Waiting for me to do something douchey, like get into a fight with the one clown over there cheering for the Leafs?"

"Oh?" Lazlo let another laugh, but this one was gentler, almost like he had been taken by surprise. "I had just been thinking that you don't seem like you're trashy. It would be cool to watch you fight that clown, though, with your lean frame."

Harrison fiddled with the small button of his flannel henley. "I'm not lean. I have some muscles hiding under here from a couple of decades of installing windows. Er, but I do have a bit of a snack belly and some really squishy love handles you probably can't see because we're sitting. My son and I mostly bond over food, so we eat a lot."

Lazlo arched an eyebrow. "Son? You didn't mention that in your profile."

"Uh, yeah." Guilt pinched Harrison as he twirled his fork around some soggy fries. "I thought no one would match with me if they thought I had a small kid running around. I should have said I'm a dad, though. Sorry."

"That's fair. I wouldn't have swiped right, because I assume dads aren't trash."

Harrison bit his lip, fighting back memories of the hurtful things his father had said and done. "You really haven't been in this world for long, have you?"

"Oh." Lazlo's curious expression flattened. "I see."

"My son's eighteen," Harrison quickly added. "In university. Good kid. Adult. Whatever. This part of my life is still very new to me. Justin just moved out a few weeks ago."

The smile returned to Lazlo's face. "Ah, you're on your own now, so you're finally dating again?"

"Kind of like that, yeah." Harrison brought the fries to his lips. "Not totally alone. Still have Tiger and Leopard."

Lazlo leaned forward. His tentacles moved forward in excitement with him. "You got a tiger and a leopard?!"

"Oh, no, those are my hamsters' names!"

Harrison tittered nervously, aware of how close one tentacle in particular was to his cheek. His chest tightened as curiosity thrummed through him. What did touching them feel like? What about touching Lazlo's skin? Or gliding his tongue along the jewels in Lazlo's mouth?

Quickly, Harrison poured himself another glass and

guzzled most of it in one go. There was no way he was getting excited about a demon.

As he set the glass down, he caught Lazlo's amused smirk. The way the demon looked at him felt so much different from how any human had ever looked at him. The easiness glowing from the demon's bright eyes sent a thrill down his stomach.

It had been a long time since Harrison had been viewed as someone besides a parent, a contractor, or a disappointing son. When he had come out to his family, the more homophobic members of his bloodline quit talking to him altogether, but things were still tense with the ones who sent him their annual Christmas cards. The only people Harrison regularly interacted with were his son and his coworkers. All of his friends from high school and trade school distanced themselves from him once he became a full-time single dad.

He liked the attention he got from Lazlo. He didn't understand the demon's existence in the least, but he was actually enjoying the date. This Valentine's Day would certainly never be forgotten.

"Looks, humor, skills, responsibility, and a totally hot way of drinking beer," Lazlo remarked. "You're not really shaping up to be trash at all."

Harrison flashed a smile, one that felt as warm as the beer surging through him. "Sorry to disappoint you. I guess you'll have to end your journey with me and continue your hunt for trashy queer men somewhere else. I'm sure there's gotta be some online."

Lazlo averted his gaze, fussing with his ponytail once more. "I don't think I would mind seeing you again, actually, although I assume that won't happen. You're fun. And it's really nice to just be myself, what with you able to see past my well-constructed magical disguise."

Ah. The hot human from the profile pic. Harrison had nearly forgotten about that.

He gestured to Lazlo's phone. "Is the picture on Maple-Mance what other people see?"

"Supposed to be. Don't know why you're the exception." Lazlo finally looked at him again. His red hair had been freed from its tie prison and now flowed messily down his shoulders. A small tentacle caressed the ends of his tresses. "But I'm kind of glad it worked out this way. It's hard pretending to be someone you're not, you know?"

Harrison's smile broadened. For a few breaths, he became acutely aware of the intense way his heart could beat.

He definitely understood. So well. And maybe it wouldn't hurt to see if he could understand more of the pleasure-turned-trash demon.

"If you feel up to another date after tonight, I'm game." Harrison held his hand to his chest in an attempt to keep his heart from jumping out of his ribcage. "For now, do you wanna order some more poutine?"

The pleased expression that unfurled across Lazlo's pretty face followed Harrison well after the date at the sports bar was over.

# CHAPTER 3

*H*arrison rolled over in bed as his phone went off. Not an alarm. He didn't work very often during the winter, as was the case for a lot of window installers in the city. Only contractors who dealt with furnaces and plumbing stayed busy when it dipped to subzero temperatures. During the lean months, the Happy Handyman head honcho called occasionally to redeploy Harrison to join a drywall or floor crew in need of another body.

This was probably one of those calls.

Harrison sat up straight when he saw the name glowing on his screen. It wasn't the boss calling—it was his son.

The usual flowchart of potential problems and solutions dangled in Harrison's brain as he answered the video call. "Hey, buddy, what's going on?"

Justin's sweet, soft brown eyes shimmered as he looked directly into the camera. "Hey, sorry, did I call at a bad time?"

Well. Nothing about Justin's easygoing voice sounded off, and he still had a healthy flush to his square, slightly doughy face. The kid wasn't panicking or had fallen ill. That was a relief.

"No, I was just sleeping." Harrison rubbed his temple, now aware of a dull, throbbing pain in his head.

"At this hour? It's almost eleven." Justin's dark brows stitched together in concern. "Are you getting sick?"

Eleven?! Harrison tapped his phone and eyed the clock. Holy crap. Most of the morning had disappeared already.

He fumbled out of bed and held the phone to his face as he headed downstairs. "No. I was out late. I didn't get in until after two, and then…"

Harrison stopped at the top of the stairs. Last night flooded him in vivid detail. Lots of beers. Lots of poutine and eventually some mozzarella sticks. Lots of time wasted trying to get past level one in a shitty hockey arcade game. Waiting outside the sports bar for a taxi to arrive. Giggling about Lazlo digging through the trash can while huge, clumpy snowflakes fell. Coming home and blasting Nickelback while talking to the hamsters, unable to sleep because he couldn't stop picturing what a second date with the demon might entail.

Date. He had had a date last night. With a demon. And enjoyed it.

That…couldn't be right.

"You were out?" Justin gasped. "Doing what? Was there an emergency at work?"

"No, no. I was, uh, you know." Harrison slowly descended the stairs, recalling the gems sparkling on Lazlo's lovely skin and the suckers wiggling along his lively tentacles. "I had a date for Valentine's, actually."

"What?!" Justin disappeared from the screen briefly, but his shoes came into view. The kid had dropped his phone.

Harrison frowned as he headed into the kitchen. "Don't be that dramatic. It was just a date."

*With a demon.*

Ugh. There was no way he had been on a date with a demon.

"No wonder you didn't call me at all yesterday." Justin came back into view. He ran his hand through his thin auburn curls. "I figured you'd hound me about my Valentine's plans at some point."

Oh. Right. Maybe he should have done that, actually. Given a casual reminder about condoms or something. As awkward as discussing Justin's sex life was, Harrison knew it was incredibly unlikely his serial dating son was still a virgin. Especially now that he didn't live at home.

"*Did* you have Valentine's plans?" Harrison opened the medicine cabinet and grabbed the painkillers. "Tell me about—"

"No, no, no." Justin lifted an eyebrow and broke into an amused smirk. One that made Harrison want to hide inside the fridge. "This is the first time you've ever told me you had a date. I want details. Did you try a dating app like I told you to?"

Harrison swallowed a pill, wishing he could swallow his phone as well. "MapleMance, yeah. I matched with him there."

"And who is he, exactly?"

Great question. Harrison bought some time by loudly clearing his throat and pouring himself a glass of water. How did one tell their son that a tall, gorgeous human messaged them for a date, but a short demon with at least a dozen tentacles showed up? He scarcely believed it himself. Maybe he had imagined the whole thing.

It really was just so absurd. A demon with a dozen or more tentacles, a laugh sharper than icicles hanging off an eavestrough, a thick body that looked nice to spoon with...

Harrison brought the glass of water to his lips. If Lazlo

had been a figment of his imagination, then why were his veins coming to life with desire?

"Damn, Dad, hurry up." Justin cackled. "What's his name? How old is he?"

Christ, is this what Harrison sounded like when he interrogated Justin on his new girlfriends? He took a long drink before answering. "His name's Lazlo. He's, uh, about my age, I guess."

*You live for a few thousand years as a pleasure demon, you kinna come from everywhere.*

Harrison treated himself to another long drink. Maybe he had invented Lazlo, after all.

"Lazlo." Justin waggled his eyebrows. "What did you do last night? Are you going to see him again?"

"Settle down." Harrison pinched the bridge of his nose. "We went to a sports bar in the southeast. And...I think we might go out again. I offered a second date."

His heart flipped as he contemplated the notion of seeing Lazlo again. Would it be a demon he saw? A human?

It was actually probably imperative to have another date with Lazlo. Just to untangle the chaos in his brain. He needed to confirm if he was dating demons in realistic daydreams or...just straight up dating demons. Hell, he'd settle for a drive-by thumbs up.

A groan rolled out of Harrison as he thought about driving. "I have to go pick up the truck. I took a cab home last night."

"Way to go, Dad. Look at you, being safe while having fun." Justin flashed him a teasing smile. "That's awesome you went out. I'm proud of you. You should definitely get that second date before someone else snatches the bearded lumberjack who made you sleep in until eleven in the morning."

"Bearded lumberjack?" Harrison couldn't help laughing. "You think that's my type?"

Justin shrugged. "I don't know. My dad doesn't talk about guys he likes, so I assume you went out with a tall dude who hasn't had a haircut in four years and tossed you a pilsner before asking if you wanted to go for a rip in his Tacoma that has big, rubbery balls dangling from the back."

Harrison shook his head, trying to mask his embarrassment. His son had quite an imagination, one the single parent had always appreciated until, well, now.

But had Justin really put much thought into the sort of man his dad would date? Shouldn't kids just worry about their own personal lives? For eighteen years, Justin had been about himself and his social circle. That was the arrangement that Harrison preferred. Parents should care for their children, not the other way around.

A familiar drop of sorrow splashed onto Harrison's tongue as he thought about his own parents and the way he used to hide everything from them in fear they would hate him. Said fears had not been unfounded.

"You're technically not wrong," Harrison confessed, drumming his fingers along the side of his glass. "I wouldn't have minded going out with a bearded lumberjack. But Lazlo isn't a bearded lumberjack. He's…"

*Humans throw away so much stuff they think is worthless. It's amazing.*

A smile danced in the corner of Harrison's mouth. "He works in waste management. He's a lot shorter than his profile indicated."

"Uh-oh. You got catfished?"

The smile stretched from ear to ear as the absurdity of the entire situation settled in. "A little. Come on, enough about me. What did *you* do last night?"

"Nothing, actually." Justin sighed and scratched his neck. "Hung out with some of the guys."

"No girls?"

"Not even a single limb of one."

Harrison snorted. "I'd be more concerned if you had part of a girl instead of a whole one."

"You know what I mean!" Justin stuck out his tongue.

"Have you heard back from the place you applied at?" Harrison asked, switching to father mode. No matter what, Justin wasn't getting out of talking about himself.

Justin, of course, dodged the question. "Okay, Dad, you're really looking rough there. You should eat a big, greasy cheeseburger. Best cure for a hangover."

"Didn't I teach you that advice when you came home drunk the summer you were sixteen?"

"Whoa, I gotta go!" Justin brought the phone close to his mouth. "Love you! See you Sunday for dinner. Give Tiger and Leopard treats for me!"

A chuckle rippled out of Harrison as he ended the call. There was no mystery about his son's ethanol expeditions, at least.

Admittedly, a cheeseburger did sound good.

Harrison scrolled through the apps on his phone to find a place that would deliver one to him as quickly as possible. After ordering a meal, he stepped outside and lit up a cigarette. Strange that his body hadn't been shaking with a nicotine craving. He couldn't recall smoking at all during the date last night, so it had been nearly eighteen hours since his last smoke.

The thought of last night motivated him to check MapleMance.

No new messages from Lazlo. His profile remained the same as last night, except the name had been updated. There was still that golden Adonis staring at him instead of the ruby, octopus-like demon.

Was it going to be weird to message him about another date? Last night, it felt like Lazlo had been very open to the idea. Was that still true today? Maybe he had just been drunk off the beer when he talked about wanting to see Harrison again. Once he sobered up, he might have realized that the human wasn't a great catch. For God's sake, there had definitely been a stretch of twenty minutes where Harrison had repeated the same joke about people thinking he worked with computers when he introduced himself as a windows installer.

Maybe it was best to leave last night where it was. One Valentine's Day with a guy he had matched with on a dating app.

Lazlo's tongue, adorned with jewels and suckers, came to mind. Harrison's throat went dry as he imagined feeling that tongue against his skin.

Correction: One Valentine's Day with a demon he had matched with on a dating app.

It was truthfully going to be disappointing if Harrison discovered he had hallucinated the whole date. There was a lot about the trash demon that was interesting. Getting to know him better would be, well, exciting. The lonely dad also wasn't opposed to more nights of coming home drunk, blasting Nickelback, and cuddling with the hamsters because he was having a good time.

Fuck it. He'd just send a message and forget about everything. If Lazlo ghosted him, then he ghosted him.

*Hey, Lazlo, I had a great time last night. Still down for another date if you are.*

There. Sent. Harrison Hamilton the Hangover Haver was smooth as butter.

After finishing his cigarette and stepping back inside, Harrison's phone buzzed. The smooth butter whipped itself into a messy meringue as he read the sweetest reply.

*I was hoping you would want to see me again, but I was too afraid to message you! When and where can we meet?*

# CHAPTER 4

*O*nce again, Harrison found himself idling in his truck, staring at the outside of a sports bar with his nerves tightening every string in his body. Different sports bar, at least. And a different colored henley.

Somehow, being in this situation was more overwhelming. After three days of replaying Valentine's Day, Harrison had decided a date had definitely happened. But whether the date had been with a handsome human or a distinctive demon would be confirmed in mere minutes.

If he was going on a second date with a human, then that meant Harrison probably needed to go to a hospital or on the waitlist for a very expensive psychiatrist.

If he was going on a second date with a demon…

He didn't really know what he was supposed to do with that knowledge. Was there an ulterior motive for demons dating humans? Were they eating more greasy food tonight because Lazlo wanted to prime him for consumption?

All right. He was a full five minutes late for his date. It would be rude to keep Lazlo waiting for a second longer.

Especially when he had seemed so excited in his messages about their date.

The second Harrison opened the door to the bar, he fully regretted a lot of things. Perhaps picking a sports bar on a Saturday night when the province's two NHL teams were duking it out on the ice wasn't his smartest decision. The place was *packed*. Chances were high of running into some shithead who wouldn't appreciate two men out on a date.

And he couldn't immediately find any tentacles. The strings inside him tightened more, and his tongue became coated with rust. It would only take a gentle breeze to break him.

"Oh, hey!" An unforgettable gravelly voice curled in his ears. "There you are."

Harrison let go of the door and spun around to meet the person talking to him. His heart swelled as he came face-to-face with a squad of crimson tentacles. He cocked his gaze downward and properly met a warm set of golden eyes and a curved, shimmery smile.

"Whoa, I forgot about how much taller you are than me." Lazlo rested a hand on his hip. "Still. Really happy to meet you out here. I went in there for a minute, but I panicked and left. A lot of you humans look the same from the back, you know?"

Harrison nodded, taking in the intangible sight before him. Yes, there was probably about six inches of vertical difference between them. Lazlo was still wearing a sideless vest, but it was a different color from the other night and had a few stains on it. There were knee-high boots on the ends of his feet (if one could call the larger tentacles legs), but one of them had a hole along the zipper. A black toque hid his mane of red hair, and a black mini-skirt covered whatever might be hiding along his center.

Was there something under there? If he had been a pleasure demon, then... No, but the tentacles could... ...couldn't they?

"You look nice," Harrison forced himself to say before his imagination got too active. "You're definitely real."

Lazlo stared at him for a long moment, and then he broke into his charmingly loud laughter. His tentacles bobbed in merriment with him. "Have you been having a bit of an existential crisis since our last date?"

"Maybe." Harrison stepped aside as a couple of people in red jerseys approached the bar. Neither of them reacted to Lazlo as they entered the building. "How do other humans react when they learn about the existence of demons?"

"Shit if I know. You're the first human I've met who could perceive the real me, remember?" Lazlo gestured to the sports bar. "Wanna go in, or should we do something else? It's really crowded. I don't like having to rein in my tentacles to the point where I'm hugging myself. *Hmm*, but there's probably a ton of good trash in there tonight."

"One hundred percent guarantee, yes." Harrison sent a silent prayer to the staff who'd have to kick out drunk hockey fans during the third quarter of the game. "But we're in a city with a million and a half people. Anywhere we go will have trash."

One of Lazlo's tentacles extended toward Harrison's cheek, but it didn't quite touch him. "I like the way you think. Any other place you wanna go to? I chose the last date. This one should be yours."

Date. Yes. They were on a date. And Harrison was about five breaths away from discovering what a demon tentacle felt like. Part of him wanted to lean in, but his proximity to the appendage didn't necessarily mean Lazlo wanted to be touched.

Besides, something about it seemed...intimate. It would be more meaningful to wait until they had gotten closer.

Or maybe it had just been a really long ass time since Harrison had gotten laid, and the mere idea of touching a good-looking guy gave him a quarter of a boner. Actually touching Lazlo would probably send him over the edge.

As the tentacle pulled away and returned to Lazlo's side, a desire to get to know the demon burned through the human. Even though now was definitely not an appropriate time to contemplate sex with a creature he barely knew.

"It doesn't really matter to me where we go," Harrison finally said. "Just seeing you is fine."

"Oh, we are quite a charmer, aren't we?" Lazlo brought his hands to his face. His tentacles also clung close to his body, with some of them wrapping around his arms. "Here I was, going into the world of online dating, thinking I'd find some good trash. Think I just found something good instead."

Heat crashed into Harrison, briefly causing him to forget they were standing outside in a subzero winter wonderland.

He fiddled with the zipper of his jacket. "Do you have any ideas of where we should go? I can drive us wherever."

"That's nice of you to offer, but I doubt your car can house me." Lazlo gestured to the tentacles. "I barely fit up front in the garbage trucks. I always prefer to hang off the back, even though I'm not supposed to do that."

"You see what I drive?" Harrison pointed to his humongous truck with the obtusely large wheels. All that was missing from making it a classic Albertan ride was the truck nuts. "You can fit. And yes, my son absolutely made fun of me when I brought it home."

It had been a bit of a silly purchase, considering Harrison drove the work van more than his own vehicle. He had owned the truck for three years and rarely took it further than the grocery store.

Lazlo's stance relaxed, and his tentacles spread out more

freely as he inspected the bed of the truck. "Oh, yeah. I could fit back here just nicely."

"I meant the front. You can't ride in the cab? There's two rows of seats."

Lazlo turned to him. Genuine mystification veiled his face. "You'd want me to ride with you?"

"Why wouldn't I? You're my date." Harrison flicked on the car ignition with his fob and unlocked it. "Get in. Tell me where we're going."

After another moment of gaping, Lazlo hopped into the passenger side of the truck. "Hop" might not have been the right verb, but "slither" didn't describe it, either. His longer tentacles grew in height, allowing his short frame to slide into the seat without a struggle.

So. Parts of Lazlo were...adjustable. That was good to know. Possibly.

Regardless, Harrison claimed his spot behind the driver's wheel. He couldn't help smiling when he noticed just how much space Lazlo took up. Several of the tentacles had found their way to the back row, which was probably the first time those seats had been touched by anything living. And Lazlo hummed with glee as he buckled in his seatbelt (after fighting a few of his appendages).

Purchasing this truck had been a good choice, after all.

Harrison strapped his own seatbelt across his torso. "What should we do?"

"I told *you* to decide."

"I'm a terrible decision maker. My son or my coworkers determine all of my meals. You should see how terribly I eat on my days off from work with Justin out of the house now." Harrison sighed. "Even during our first date, I let you do all the ordering."

Lazlo chuckled. "Not after two pitchers of beers. You aggressively ordered more drinks and mozzarella sticks. And you were whimpering about them now having some kind of donair pizza. Remember?"

Harrison rubbed the back of his increasingly warm neck. "Actually, no. I just remember shoving all that into my maw. I thought that was you."

"Nope. All you. And all the arcade games we played. Never seen anyone go through loonies like you."

Really? Huh. Drunk Harrison sounded like fun.

"Seat warmers?" Lazlo leaned back and removed his toque. "These are nice. Luxurious. So, yeah, what do you like to do? What are your hobbies? Start driving. Let's get on the road."

It should have been easy to answer, but nothing came to mind. Not a single activity. For the last ten years, Harrison had raised his son and installed windows in buildings. There was little room for any personal pursuits. Even now, he couldn't think of what he used to like to do.

Although, truthfully, all the things he used to do before the divorce were to appease his parents, ex-wife, and very heterosexual high school friends—hunting, fishing, clubbing, playing sports. The only activity he had retained from his closeted days was sports, but only from the comfort of his couch with some takeout Chinese and a few cheap beers.

Harrison pulled out of the parking lot, not wishing to dwell much more on his past. "I listen to music, I guess."

"Yeah? Like who?"

"Nickelback." In the past, Harrison wouldn't have dared to tell anyone. But right now, with Lazlo, it seemed safe to make the confession. "They're an Albertan band. Lot of people consider them bad, but they're my favorite group."

"Really? Nice!" Not a trace of judgment clouded Lazlo's response, which stirred hope inside Harrison that he wasn't coming off as weird. "Can we make a Nickelback date?"

"Uh, I don't know." Harrison gripped the steering wheel.

"None of my interests make for good dates unless they're playing live, I guess. Like hockey. I enjoy watching it, but I don't know if watching hockey in a bar is a good date idea. Not unless we were in the stadium."

"Shame we're not. That place has good garbage. Huge bins outside devoted to old popcorn."

That wasn't a surprise to hear. Harrison turned onto the main road. Not too many cars on the roads. No ice. Not an obscene amount of salt, either. No ice. Excellent driving conditions for a Saturday night in February.

"I guess I like driving too," Harrison added. "Haven't had much company in my truck before. If it wasn't so late and still very much winter, I'd say we should go for a rip."

"A rip? Bong rip? I'm game."

"No, the other kind of rip." Harrison patted his dashboard. "This truck can go off-roading like a champion. Allegedly. I haven't tried it yet with this truck. Weed's not totally off the table, though. You smoke, eh?"

Lazlo's hearty laugh filled the truck with a new layer of warmth. "You Canadians. Really precious. So, where are we going?"

Harrison grinned and tried to ignore the sinking feeling in his heart that this date was a disaster because he was as exciting as cardboard. It was obvious the two weren't going to *go* anywhere.

"We could hit a drive-thru," Harrison suggested, secretly wishing there was a place with donair pizza nearby. Now that Lazlo had reminded him of its existence, he wanted something sweet and savory. But that might not have suited the demon's tastes. Donair pizza barely suited most humans' tastes. "Monahan's?"

"Yeah, let's do that! Going for a drive and hitting shit? That sounds awesome."

Harrison chuckled. "I'm not sure we're picturing the same

definition of hitting the drive-thru, but as long as we don't get in trouble, I guess I'm open to being flexible."

"You're on a date with a demon. I assumed a long time ago you were very flexible."

Something about the inflection of Lazlo's tone bordered on sultry. Harrison stole a glance at his date and found the lackadaisical demon looking back at him, a smirk carved into his intriguing face. His eyes glowed with promises, and the gems on his body and entwined in his hair had a unique sparkle to them. Even the tentacles had taken on a particular sheen that made them quite inviting.

The two only looked at each other for a moment, but it was enough to remind Harrison that Lazlo was a pleasure demon. One who clearly knew how to seduce someone. Or, at least, he knew how to seduce a certain contractor with empty nest syndrome.

Christ, what was said contractor with empty nest syndrome even thinking? Lazlo had pointedly said the other night that sex bored him. He hadn't even mentioned if he was interested in romance with anyone. Just that he had been looking for a trashy man.

Right. Harrison turned his eyes back to the road. They were on a date now, yes, but there was no indication that Lazlo's intentions centered anything but trash. Some kind words and eager messages on a dating app didn't inherently carry a particular meaning.

And, well, it was probably ridiculous to toy with the notion of doing anything with a demon. Honestly, he probably shouldn't have been doing *this*.

"What's on your mind?" Lazlo asked. "Or do you need me to keep quiet so you can focus? Seems like there are all kinds of drivers. I haven't figured out who falls into what category."

"You categorize drivers?"

"Oh, for sure. I categorize everything, buddy."

Harrison chuckled. "You sound like you've been living in Alberta your whole life."

"I'm trying to learn the inner quirks of the English spoken here. Same for Punjabi since I work with a lot of great Pakistani people."

"You speak Punjabi?"

"I inherently speak every language. Part of being a pleasure demon. You pick up the language instantly in new realms. Makes for better communication." A titter rolled out of Lazlo. "Wouldn't do to enter horny people's beds with so many tentacles and no way to reassure them you're not going to strangle them. Unless they're into breathplay. Which some humans and demons and other beings that I don't think I should talk about are."

Breathplay?

Harrison's gaze darted toward the tentacles briefly. Instantly, he realized he should not let his mind go down that path while he was driving. "Uh, we're almost at a Monahan's. What do you want to eat?"

"Drive by the big bin there real slow, then I'll decide."

Lazlo pointed to the dumpster in the corner of the fairly empty Monahan's parking lot. Obediently, Harrison went straight for it. Instead of driving by, though, he parked in front of the bin and left the ignition running.

"Oh, yeah, you totally get it, don't you?" Enthusiasm colored Lazlo's voice as he hopped out of the truck. "Wanna look with me?"

Harrison shrugged and decided to get out of the truck. Not like he had to touch anything. And there was plenty of hand sanitizer in the truck.

Besides, watching Lazlo's tentacles dig through the thin slot of the locked bin was quite a spectacle. The demon's fingers spun the dial of the combination lock, and determination brewed in his wide-eyed, tense expression.

"Gotta move fast in places like this," Lazlo explained. "Considering people throw away their stuff, they sure get upset when anyone digs through their trash."

"Yeah, I never understood that." Harrison pulled out his pack of smokes. "My neighbors have a security camera pointed at their bins. Guess they're threatened by the old lady who searches the recycling for bottles and cans."

By now, Lazlo had his back turned away from Harrison completely. "You got a dame like that on your street? She sounds fun."

Harrison stuck a cigarette in his mouth and lit it. "I don't know if she does it for fun. Pretty sure she just collects things that are worth money at the bottle depot."

"Maybe she has also fun. How could she not?" One of Lazlo's tentacles held up a long sheet of metal. "Look at this thing! What is it? Why'd they throw it away?"

Lazlo slid it back in the bin before Harrison could venture a guess. The human who was quite out of his element opted to smoke quietly and watch his date.

The demon's attention to the combination lock hadn't waned in the least, but the tentacles started pulling out more stuff. Empty egg cartons, greasy napkins, broken coffee containers, knives without handles, and so forth. All trash. But Lazlo didn't seem to want to keep anything.

"What do you do when you're looking through the trash?" Harrison asked. "Do you, uh, categorize it?"

Lazlo kept his back to Harrison. The tentacles pulled out some squished paper cups. "Sure do. Damn, this is a tricky lock. Doesn't take long to guess the combo with three numbers, but a fourth digit really—"

"What are you doing?" An unfamiliar voice broke through the strange, crisp night air.

Oh, shit. Harrison turned on his heel to face the new person, effectively blocking them from viewing Lazlo. The red collared shirt and stained baseball cap indicated they worked at Monahan's. The trash bag in their grasp meant that Harrison and Lazlo were fated to meet this minimum wage employee.

Fortunately, they were, like, sixteen. Teenagers weren't jumping at the chance to call the cops. And Harrison wasn't afraid of anyone who wasn't old enough to vote. Not after taking Justin to the hospital because he had broken his arm while copying a social media trend to eat spaghetti while jumping on a trampoline.

Harrison held up his cigarette. "Sorry. Just wanted to have a smoke before I grabbed a bite to eat. I don't like to smoke in my truck, and I didn't want to bother anyone in the parking lot."

The...very empty parking lot.

The employee attempted to peer around Harrison, but he moved his arm holding the cigarette in some attempt to protect Lazlo. Visibly (and rightfully) annoyed, the employee walked around Harrison and approached the dumpster.

To Harrison's relief, Lazlo had hopped back in the truck. The demon waved to Harrison with one of his tentacles as he covered his hands in sanitizer.

Harrison took one last drag and then put out his smoke under his boot. "Now I'm all done!"

"Okay," replied the employee. "Just, uh, get going. I guess."

"You don't get paid enough to deal with people like me, huh?" Harrison punctuated his question with a polite chuckle. "Sorry, again. I was in the way. Hope you have a good shift."

"Uh, thanks. Hope you have a good, er, meal."

"Will do!"

Harrison quickly jumped into his still-running truck. "Hope you haven't changed your mind about eating here, because now we definitely have to."

"Holy crap." Lazlo handed him the bottle of sanitizer. "That was hot."

The bluntness of the statement threw Harrison off-guard. He fumbled with buckling his seatbelt while trying to grab the bottle. "Er, what was?"

Lazlo leaned against the dashboard and flashed him a smile that sparkled more than the gems on his skin. "You. Covering for me."

While Harrison technically heard the response, it was difficult to believe anyone found anything he did as hot. But it was very warm in the truck, more than it should have been. He fanned his neck, suddenly desiring a chance to make snow angels outside.

"And let me be honest about something." Lazlo's tongue swiped his lower lip as he ran a hand through his hair. "Watching you do something trashy like smoke is really, really hot."

One of Lazlo's tentacles brushed against Harrison's thigh. The human's gaze veered downward as his imagination grew wild with suggestions of where else the tentacle could touch him.

Harrison bit his lip, forcing himself to meet Lazlo's expression. The demon's golden eyes had a soft glow to them, and his playful smile held so much sincerity to them. All the tentacles wiggling around in the truck seemed to be pointing at the flustered human.

There was a lot about the demon that was memorable, but the way he made Harrison's heart race with a single glance had to be at the top of the list of unforgettable traits.

Neither of them knew why Harrison could perceive the real Lazlo. But in that moment, the human was quite glad he could see past the smoke and mirrors.

Slowly, Harrison rested his hand on the tentacle closest to him. It was softer than he had expected, but just as smooth as he had anticipated. While tempting to curl his fingers around the appendage and find out what the suckers felt like, he decided this light touch would be enough for now. The way Lazlo didn't pull away suggested he was fine with the arrangement too.

With Lazlo's tentacle on his lap and his hand over the appendage, Harrison headed for the drive-thru to start the next part of their date.

# CHAPTER 5

*I*t had only been a few weeks since Harrison had last seen Justin in person, so he found himself unexpectedly touched by the sight of his grown child rushing into the house and making a beeline for the hamsters.

"No hugs for your old man?" Harrison slid onto the couch and opened the food delivery app on his phone. While he craved a donair pizza, it would be better to let Justin decide on the menu. He wanted his kid to eat exactly what he wanted to eat. "All right. I see how it is. I'll just have dinner by myself."

Justin—had he grown taller?—loomed by the hamster cages with Leopard in his arms. "You know how much I missed these babies."

"But not me?" Harrison laughed. "Which one of us is paying for your education?"

"You know I missed you too! But you can video call me anytime you want. These cuties can't." Justin stuck out his tongue.

Harrison lifted an eyebrow. "Anytime? I seem to recall a

certain teenager asking me not to call him on Friday and Saturday nights in case he's out on a date."

Justin left his tongue dangling for another minute. A cheesy smile unfurled across his face as he rolled the tongue back up. "Wanna do tacos for dinner?"

"Yeah, that sounds good." Harrison flipped to the Tex-Mex section of restaurant choices. There was only one place the Hamiltons ever ordered from when it came to tacos. "Should we get the usual? Or do you want something different?"

"What do you do when you're out with Lazlo?"

Harrison froze in place and kept his gaze on his phone screen. Great. They were talking about Lazlo already.

Justin put Leopard back in her cage and flopped on the other end of the couch. His teasing eyes and tight smile meant there was no way Harrison was going to avoid talking about his dating life.

But how did one talk about a demon he had no actual relationship with?

"Why are you interested in my personal business?" Harrison busied himself once more with ordering dinner. "We've only gone out twice."

"Yeah, and what have you two done? Probably just eat, right?" Justin waggled his eyebrows. "Does Lazlo order food for you?"

Harrison finished placing the order, including a generous tip. "Hope you wanted the usual spicy chicken tacos with poutine because you didn't tell me otherwise what you wanted."

"So that's a yes." Justin grabbed a couch cushion and held it close to his chest. "Come on, Dad. You gotta be really exciting on dates if you wanna keep seeing this Lazlo. Take some initiatives. You got any pics of him? Let me see who my new daddy is."

41

A burst of heat threatened to choke Harrison. "Whoa, settle down! Like I said, we've only gone out twice. And we are definitely not close enough for you to worry about getting an additional father. We haven't even discussed a third date."

Justin held out his hand. "You met him on MapleMance? Show me his profile. He's got pictures there, doesn't he?"

Sigh. Perhaps it would be best to give in to Justin's demands. The sooner they got the awkwardness of Lazlo out of the way, the sooner they could focus on the questions burning through Harrison—like if Justin was doing well in his classes or if he had joined any new clubs or started dating a new girl.

Pushing back the memories of last night—of holding Lazlo's tentacle for as long as possible in the drive-thru and feeling giddy about every moment of it—Harrison opened the MapleMance app. Once he had Lazlo's profile pulled up, he passed the phone to Justin.

Justin flopped onto his back as he scrolled through the profile. "Damn, Dad. You're telling me someone who looks like *this* went out with you?"

*Well, not quite.*

Harrison frowned as the second half of Justin's observation sunk in. "What's wrong with me?"

"Nothing. I just figured someone named Lazlo would look like a squid."

At once, Harrison covered his mouth and hoped the rest of his expression didn't reveal too much.

"In all fairness, you're also my dad and not the gender I like, so I don't think much about dating you." Justin blew him a kiss as he handed the phone back. "He really looks like that, huh?"

"There might be a filter or two…"

"But you like how he looks in person?" Justin sat up. "That's all that matters."

"That's not *all* that matters." Harrison's heart skipped a beat as he recalled the luxurious sheen to Lazlo's tentacles and the thickness of his upper arms. "But I do like how he looks."

Yes, he was physically attracted to a demon. So what? Not like he was going to be able to tell anyone that.

"When is date three happening?" Justin picked up the remote from the coffee table and turned on the television.

"Don't know if it's even happening. Can you mind your own business yet?"

Instantly, Justin turned off the television. He turned to Harrison. "Uh-uh. You dating someone *is* my business."

The humor in his son's voice had disappeared. There was a Conversation with a capital C about to happen. Usually, those only happened when Justin was in trouble about something. Harrison's stomach clenched itself as he braced himself to be on the receiving end of a Conversation.

"Not a single time while you were raising me did you go out with anyone," Justin said. "I've been worried about you're going to do without me in the house. You're allowed to live your life and maybe even fall in love, you know? I don't need you to be my dad all the time anymore."

Harrison kept to his end of the couch and listened quietly. There were some lovely, mature sentences dancing out of Justin's mouth. Lots of good, valid points.

But it was hard to deny the last sentence in particular hurt.

He didn't have anyone he really called family except Justin. His mother called once in a while and judged the hell out of him for not suddenly making up with his piece of shit homophobic father. Some cousins and a lone uncle messaged every now and then. But his family—his life—was Justin.

Maybe Justin didn't need Harrison as much anymore. That had to be why he wanted to push his dad away. Justin was ready to live his own life. That was probably how things should be.

But Harrison still needed Justin. That truth encompassed him so viscerally, he couldn't stand another moment of facing it.

He rose from the couch. "I'm going to step out for a smoke. You should get some drinks for us. No beers if you're going to drive back to campus tonight."

Justin glared at him. "And I bet you're going to come back in and pretend I didn't say any of that."

"I'm going to come back in and look for a hockey game for us to watch." Harrison grabbed his cigarettes and lighter from the coffee table. "Or I can stand here until you tell me about the job you applied for a while back."

"At least message Lazlo and ask him out on another date if you like him." Justin huffed, clutching the couch cushion. "Don't wait for him to say something. Dating isn't about that wait-three-days-before-calling thing the cavepeople in your time did. Just go for what you like! That's what I do."

"And how well does that work out for you?" Harrison forced himself to smile. "One of us had a Valentine's date, and I don't believe it was you."

Justin threw the cushion at his father, but he (hopefully intentionally) missed.

A moment later, Harrison stood outside and silently enjoyed the first drag of his cigarette. He tried not to think about anything, but Justin's words kept echoing through him.

*I don't need you to be my dad all the time anymore.*

What was he supposed to be now? There wasn't much else to him underneath the dad bod and calloused hands, as last night's date had shown. Couldn't even think of anything to do because he had no real hobbies or interests.

Eventually, Harrison found himself looking at Maple-Mance again. Specifically, at his messages with Lazlo. The demon had sent him a couple of heart-eye emojis after the date, and Harrison had said he wanted to meet up again, but there had been nothing else since.

In this moment, Harrison could feel how very dull he was. And it wasn't like he could magically become an interesting person.

His chest grew warm as parts of last night rushed back to him. Lazlo smiling at him like he was, in fact, quite fun to be around. The way touching Lazlo had been exhilarating. Taking two hours to eat a meal in the truck that should have been finished in ten minutes. Pacing the floors after coming home to see if the demon would message him back.

Maybe Lazlo's feelings toward the human were neutral, but Harrison sure liked him. That much was obvious.

If pursuing a demon was what Harrison needed to do to fill the void left by the changes in his life, then...

*Hey, I was just thinking about you. Want to go out again? I don't have any ideas about what to do, but I just want to spend time with you.*

Ugh. That was way too cringey, but Harrison pressed send anyway. Better to be honest and get ghosted for it than to pretend he was some kind of chill, suave Casanova.

While putting out his cigarette, he received a reply that made him forget how to breathe.

*Should I show you some real pleasure?*

# CHAPTER 6

*T*he next night, Harrison picked up Lazlo from the place he claimed was his house, but it seemed more like a poorly crafted tent under a bridge. Not that he was the only one with a makeshift home along the Bow River.

Harrison could barely speak as he greeted the demon. The only thing he had been thinking about all day had been that particular message from Lazlo.

*Should I show you some real pleasure?*

Where were they going to go? What were they going to do? And did Harrison need to stop somewhere to buy some lube?

It didn't help that Lazlo climbed into the truck wearing an ebony latex shirt and matching shorts that barely covered any of his lower body. His wide, bare thighs (okay, tentacles) looked like they needed someone's face between them, worshiping every inch of the appendages with their tongue and lips.

If that person could be Harrison, he would be quite willing to suck whatever went into his mouth.

Harrison loudly cleared his thought, as if his horny thoughts would disappear with the action. "It's nice to see you."

"I was just about to say the same." Lazlo had his attention trained in the direction of Harrison's exposed collarbone. "Excellent henley. No coat?"

"It's in the back. It gets kind of warm in here sometimes."

Lazlo grinned. "Good."

God, was Harrison actually going to get laid tonight? He really hoped so. The prospect of his first time with a man was terrifying enough that it didn't matter said man was a demon.

A *pleasure* demon.

"You'll need it where we're going since you humans get cold easily," Lazlo added.

Harrison blinked. "Will I?"

That...didn't sound like something sexy. But maybe Lazlo wanted to try fucking outdoors when it was well below freezing. Harrison didn't mind submitting to a demon's unusual desires when said demon made his body temperature rise to new heights. A little hypothermia might be worth the risk.

"Where are we going?" Harrison pulled out the GPS navigation on his phone, eager to start the date. "Tell me the address."

Once on the way—to a part of the city that seemed suspiciously familiar—Lazlo started humming a song. It only took a few notes to recognize the yearning ballad.

Harrison glanced sidelong at Lazlo, his heart aflutter. "Have you been listening to Nickelback?"

"Yeah! This internet thing is so great. I checked out every song I could find and enjoyed some ads about yogurt in the process. I had to so I could learn more about you, you know?"

Really?

Harrison bit his lip. There didn't seem to be any judgment shadowing Lazlo's words. Most people were quick to shut down the group and their songs.

"You liked the music?" Harrison cautiously asked.

"Oh, yeah. They're sentimental and passionate. I see why you like them."

While tempting to ask for more information, Harrison decided to drive quietly and listen to Lazlo hum. Every low, muffled note from the demon hit the human's ears perfectly and gave his groin a lot of hope about what rest of the date would entail.

Passionate. That surely meant something.

Somehow, it shouldn't have surprised Harrison when they arrived at the city dump. No one around but a million birds and a staunch scent that permeated through the truck's windows.

Right. He was on a date with a pleasure-turned-trash demon. Banging horny humans had grown boring.

"I don't think we're supposed to be here at this hour," Harrison mumbled, trying to mask his disappointment.

Lazlo gestured to a gated area. "Go that way. I got a key to let us in."

Harrison rolled up to the gate's entrance. "Guess you come here often?"

"Not supposed to, but yes, I do. Can you lower the window down for me?"

"You're not supposed to come here often?" Harrison pressed the button for the passenger's side window. "I thought since you mentioned riding in garbage trucks that you come here frequently."

Lazlo's tentacles slithered out of the window, with one of them holding a small key. "I do, but not because I'm supposed to. My actual job is at the treatment plant. I just sneak onto trucks and catch rides here sometimes."

"Oh. Okay."

Once the fence was unlocked, Lazlo motioned for Harrison to drive ahead and where to turn when the road branched into two. After a few minutes of careful navigating, they reached an area filled with broken furniture, birds, and bird shit.

They parked in front of one particularly large pile of garbage. With the way Lazlo cackled as he zoomed out of the truck, one would think he was a child with free rein inside a toy store. Naturally, Harrison followed after grabbing his coat.

He left the vehicle running so the headlights could keep him from stumbling into a pit of jagged glass—and so they could make a quick escape if need be. There were a number of construction vehicles doing something on the other side of the dump. Surely, the pair would be spotted eventually.

"This is exactly what I thought it would be like!" Lazlo's tentacles went to work sorting items at the top of the pile. "You know whose garbage this is?"

Harrison stood behind Lazlo and finished zipping up his coat. "Not a clue."

"Samantha's."

"Samantha who?"

A tentacle brought a stack of signs advertising a clearance sale and waved them in front of Harrison. "Samantha's! The fashion outlet that just went out of business."

"Oh. Never been there." Harrison tilted his head to the side. Most of the junk the tentacles were pulling out were flyers or partitions. "Figured there'd be clothes."

"*Those* get destroyed somewhere fancy to ensure no one

pilfers any perfectly fine clothes, and then they get sent here to be turned into a hill with the other garbage." Lazlo peered over his shoulder. "You wanna get in on this? I'll move aside—"

"I'll watch. I don't have my safety gear in this truck." Harrison folded his arms across his chest. "And it's really cold. I presume you aren't bothered by this temperature? Not even the bravest of Albertans wear bondage gear outside when it's frostbite-along-the-ears season."

"Bondage gear?" Lazlo looked at his outfit. "Is that what this is? I just thought it was a cute outfit. Who'd throw away perfectly good threads like this? It's very stain resistant."

Harrison snorted.

"But to answer your question, I don't get cold when I'm excited." Lazlo shimmied to the right and bent down to inspect something on the ground. His tentacles kept working the top of the pile. "I only get cold when I'm doing something boring. Like waiting for the train at a station that's just been picked clean."

Harrison chuckled. "Usually people want clean train stations."

"Well, those people are lucky. The city is killing it lately in the cleanliness department along my route to work."

"Wish they would come to my neighborhood. The bus stops are always a mess there."

Lazlo stood up and turned to Harrison, holding something in his hand. "Check out these buttons. They're pretty. Guess someone forgot to send these with the clothes to the fancy shredding party."

Six metal buttons gleamed in Lazlo's palm. They weren't anything special, but the demon admired them like they were more precious than the gems dangling from his hair. A grin danced on Harrison's face as he studied Lazlo's soft expression.

Were many demons this gentle or so interested in useless things like discarded buttons?

"What's so special about trash like this for you?" Harrison asked.

"People just throw away stuff and declare it all junk. But it's not. It's still stuff that deserves proper categorization." Lazlo brought his hand close to Harrison's waist. "Can you keep these buttons in your pocket for now? I might find what they belong to later."

As much as Harrison didn't want to touch the buttons, he couldn't turn down such a simple request. As he pocketed them, Lazlo turned his full attention back to the pile of junk.

Harrison inched forward so he could be closer to Lazlo. "You try to put things back together you find in the trash?"

"No. I just categorize. But if I can see the full context of objects, I can categorize better."

There did seem to be some kind of system going on. By now, the large garbage pile had splintered into different piles. Papers, posters, and receipts were sloppily heaped together with some busted mannequins. Nearby, steel partitions and plastic hangers were stacked on top of each other.

"What kind of categories do you? Big and small?" Harrison studied the piles. "Compostable and recyclable?"

"No, nothing that overwhelming. My categories change, but I keep them simple." Lazlo pointed to the partitions. "That's 'things that people never knew they were looking at in the store.' The posters there are 'things that people knew they were looking at in the store.'"

Ah. That was quite a tidy division. Logical. No wonder Lazlo didn't know what to do with the buttons.

Harrison kicked at a mannequin's arm. "Just looking through junk and categorizing garbage brings you joy?"

"Yeah! Isn't the dump the greatest place to be?"

"For you, maybe."

"I get that a lot." Lazlo directed his attention to the pile with the papers. His hands riffled through the flyers. "Did you know they used to call the dump the 'nuisance ground?' Terrible name."

"Still do in some parts of Canada. I think mainly Saskatchewan." Harrison fished his cigarettes out of his pocket. "When I was a kid, the dump was pretty fun. Less security back then, so my sister and I would go wild throwing stuff out of the truck. The more breakable, the better. And we used to chase the birds."

"What's the deal with your sister? You haven't mentioned her much."

Lazlo's tentacles kept searching through the garbage, but the rest of him turned to Harrison. Though he was crouched by soggy cardboard boxes with the truck's headlights bouncing off his gems eerily, there was something intimate about the curiosity chiseled in the demon's bright eyes. Something that made it seem safe for Harrison to share a part of his painful past.

"Well." Harrison lit a cigarette. "We don't talk anymore. I don't really talk to my family except for my son."

The rest of Lazlo stopped searching the trash. His tentacles drooped to his sides as he rose to his feet. "Why?"

Harrison averted his gaze as he took a long drag. "They don't approve of me being gay."

"Wow, that's a garbage family you got there. Except for your son, I presume."

"Justin's great." Harrison lowered his voice. "What would I have done all these years without him?"

He glanced back at Lazlo and was startled to see how close the two had physically become. Only an arm's length apart. If that.

Lazlo's lovely lips curved downward. "And you said he's at university now? Away from you?"

"Not too far, fortunately. Across the city. But I guess some days it feels like he's on the other side of Canada." Harrison clenched his jaw, recalling yesterday's conversation with Justin. "And he doesn't really need me anymore."

"I'm sorry."

The pair fell into a silence, but it wasn't an entirely uncomfortable one. Having Lazlo so near while a familiar pain throbbed through Harrison was actually quite comforting.

Eventually, the silence was broken by a coughing fit from the human with a bad habit.

"Sorry." Harrison pounded his chest, willing his damaged lungs to knock it off. "I should quit smoking."

The smile returned to Lazlo's face. "Probably. But damn, you turn extra hot when you're engaged in trashy activities."

It was hard to believe someone like Lazlo actually found him attractive, but Harrison wanted to lean into the moment and flirt some more. Do anything except dwell on his family.

"Should I jump into a pile of garbage?" Harrison stamped out his cigarette under his boot. "Is that how I become a supermodel in your eyes? Covering myself in discarded partitions from bankrupted fashion outlets, waiting to be categorized?"

Lazlo smirked, but he didn't say anything. A challenge brimmed in his intrigued expression. A new fire encompassed Harrison, one that started from his mouth and traveled down to his groin. The only way to fully extinguish the flame would be to make his body so hot that he turned into stardust.

It was tempting to sink before Lazlo and beg the demon to have his way with him.

But they hadn't come here for sex. And there truthfully wasn't going to be a time Harrison would be so horny that he'd suck off a demon in a smelly dump.

Maybe.

"Well, I might disappoint you tonight," Harrison confessed. "I don't really want to jump into this sea of undiscovered treasure. Some birds might peck at me for food."

"You do look quite tasty," Lazlo commented, chuckling at the end of his sentence. He resumed digging through the mannequins.

"Do I...?"

Harrison crouched down next to Lazlo and pretended to be interested in the jungle of plastic limbs. Okay, they were actually cool to look at. Useless, but cool.

"Is this how you pictured our date to go?" Lazlo held up an arm.

Harrison picked up another mannequin's arm and brought it to Lazlo's, making the hands high five each other. "Not at all. But I like hanging out with you."

A sweet smile spread across Lazlo's face. Several of his tentacles high-fived the plastic hand in Harrison's grasp. "What did you think we were going to do?"

"I don't know." Harrison dropped the arm and rubbed the back of his neck. "Since you're a pleasure demon, when you told me you want to show me some real pleasure, I guess I thought we would do, uh, other things."

Lazlo studied him for a long moment. "And you were okay doing 'other things' with me?"

"I guess? That's inappropriate to admit, isn't it?" He couldn't quell the nervous laughter that rippled out of him. "Sorry. I know you find sex boring now. I'll temper my expectations for the next date."

"We're going out again?"

The surprise coloring Lazlo's question sent a new kind of heat through Harrison, one composed entirely of sheer embarrassment. He stumbled as he quickly got back on his feet.

Christ, of course it was too soon to bring up a fourth date. Especially after Harrison had just admitted he wanted to fuck Lazlo when the demon had been upfront about his disinterest in sex. Lazlo probably thought of Harrison as some kind of prick now.

"Sorry. I shouldn't have assumed." Harrison turned to his vehicle. They probably needed to leave soon, anyway, before the truck's battery died. "Maybe we should get—"

Something wrapped around Harrison's waist. The touch was light, but it sent a shiver down Harrison's spine. He glanced to meet the tentacle holding him. His heart swelled with delight, knowing Lazlo was touching him.

A moment later, the rest of the demon was right by his side. "You want to go out again? Really? After I brought you here?"

Harrison faced him directly, although he felt a pang of emptiness when Lazlo pulled his tentacle away. "I do."

"Really?" Lazlo swiped his tongue along his lower lip and broke into a bright grin. "All right. Then I don't need to wait on MapleMance for you to say something. We're going out again."

"We are." Harrison bit the inside of his cheek, enjoying the way he barely noticed that they were in a dump in the middle of winter when Lazlo smiled at him like that. "We can keep going out until you don't want to anymore. I like you."

"You do?" Lazlo broke into a boisterous laughter. "You're really hard to categorize."

Hard to categorize? What did that mean?

"Okay, we'll see how long you like me for," Lazlo added. "I promise the novelty of me being a demon will wear off soon."

That...wasn't why Harrison liked Lazlo, was it?

Then again, would he really be out here with another human for a date? But why would a human want to break into the city dump for a romantic evening?

Lazlo must have sensed the conflict inside Harrison—or possibly read it from his face. The demon ambled to the passenger side of the truck and opened the door. "Let's sanitize and go home. I gotta work early in the morning."

Yeah, that was fair. And Harrison actually had a job site to go to tomorrow. Some rich people in the northwest part of the city wanted their windows redone while they went on vacation to Arizona.

As they drove out of the dump, something warm brushed against Harrison's thigh. He didn't hesitate to grasp the appendage, allowing his fingers to curl around the soft, animated suckers. They were a bit ticklish at first, but Harrison enjoyed the strange sensation.

The demon said nothing as Harrison draped the tentacle across his lap, but he didn't pull away. In fact, the human caught a pleased expression out of the corner of his eye.

Did Lazlo like him too? Or did he just like the physical contact?

Right now, it didn't matter. Driving back to downtown while touching Lazlo and basking in his warmth was enough.

# CHAPTER 7

*H*arrison stared at the numbers he had written down. Everything had been measured properly, but he couldn't make sense of anything he was looking at.

He pulled down his goggles and rubbed his eyes. Maybe he needed to take a break before using the circular saw. His days of only sleeping for four hours and being a functioning member of society were long over.

The lack of sleep had been totally worth it. He had gotten home from his date close to two in the morning, and his body had refused to slumber until he could no longer recall the warmth of Lazlo's tentacle against his palm. Everything about last night had been wonderful.

But this morning...

*I promise the novelty of me being a demon will wear off soon.*

Those words kept bothering Harrison, though he tried his best to focus on work. Dating men in general was still very new to him—dating one who was an actual demon required him to reprogram his brain.

After grabbing his water bottle, he stepped outside. The

frosty wind instantly smacked him in the face. Pulling down his mask to take a drink was like asking Mother Nature for a fight.

"Ayyyy, Hamtaro!"

Gary's grating voice traveled along the wind, smacking Harrison with an equally insulting persistence. Mere breaths later, his coworker was at his side, holding out his hand.

"Can I bum a smoke?" he asked.

Sigh. At least Harrison was physically more awake. Being cold and irritated did wonders for the body.

Harrison removed two cigarettes from his pack and placed one in Gary's hand. He lit up his own, and then gingerly allowed Gary to borrow his lighter.

"You're so quiet this morning," Gary remarked. "Look like total dog shit too. No offense."

"Fuck off," Harrison mumbled, snatching his lighter back before Gary 'lost' it. Like the six hundred other lighters. "I just didn't get much sleep."

"No?" Gary broke into a cocky smirk. "Did you have a date?"

Harrison took a long drag before responding, knowing very well that the truth was going to mean an even more annoying version of Gary.

But he also kind of wanted to talk about Lazlo with someone. The warmth that spread through his chest at the mere thought of his unusual companion made it easy to forget the painful frost in his nostrils.

"I did," he answered. "Got home late."

"You got lucky, huh?" Gary cackled. "See. Told you that there is so much ass to conquer on dating apps."

Harrison rolled his eyes. "I didn't get 'lucky,' and if I did, it wouldn't be any of your business."

"Oh, he's playing hard to get? I know that type. I got

about six women who are playing the long game with me." Gary waggled his eyebrows. "Those are the freakiest babes."

The chances that those same six women were catfishing him were incredibly high, knowing Gary, but Harrison decided to keep that observation to himself. For now, he just wanted to drink his water and get at least half a cigarette in before his nipples became hard enough to cut a window.

"Is this the same guy you showed me?" Gary asked.

"It is."

"Damn. He's really making you work for it. Well, good for you." Gary coughed as he exhaled. "Once you fuck him, you're gonna be a new man. You'll be so confident that you'll be picking up all the gay men online."

Harrison shot him a glare. "Why do you act like I'm looking to sleep around?"

Gary lifted an eyebrow. "Aren't you? Why would you go to MapleMance if you weren't? That's for hot, sticky sex. You want something boring like marriage, you go to... Uh..."

"Nevermind." Harrison put out his cigarette in the snow. He had not slept enough to deal with both the frigid outdoors and Greasy Gary. "I'm not looking for marriage, but dating isn't just about sex for me."

"Really?" The judgment coating Gary's voice was thick enough to destroy the house's foundation.

"Really. I like hanging out with this guy." Harrison slipped the remainder of his cigarette into his pack and opened his water bottle. "That's enough, isn't it?"

"If you say so."

Lacking the energy to argue, Harrison guzzled half of his water. As he closed the bottle, his phone began ringing. Quickly—and thrilled to have an excuse to abandon Gary— he stepped back inside.

He answered his phone as he kicked the snow off his

boots. Justin's sweet, goofy face graced his screen, bringing a smile to Harrison's own tired mug.

"Hey, buddy, what's up?"

"I got the job!" Justin unleashed a train of obnoxious, happy noises. "Your son is employed!"

"That's great!" Harrison's grin broadened. He took his time returning to his station. "Tell me about it. It's not going to interfere with your classes, is it?"

"No, it's a night job. I'm going to be a barback at this place downtown."

"A club?" Harrison withheld his urge to groan. If it was *that* cowboy-themed one in particular he was thinking of, he knew Justin's checks would go straight back to the establishment.

"No, a brand new bar. They're opening next week. Mustard Point."

"Mustard?" Harrison set his water bottle down and glanced at the numbers he had scribbled down earlier. They still floated off the scrap paper he had used. "You don't mean 'muster?'"

Justin laughed. "No. Mustard is an important part of old cowboy slang. It means, like, talking a lot or something."

While Harrison started to express his doubts about the bar's name, someone's power drill kept his words from ever reaching Justin's ears. For the best, probably.

"Sorry, you're busy with work, aren't you?" A sliver of guilt crossed Justin's expression. "I'll let you go. I just wanted to tell you."

"No, no, I wanna hear more." Harrison gestured to the area behind him. "But yeah, it's kind of noisy here. Sorry. When do you start?"

"Tonight!" Justin beamed once more. "They're gonna show me where everything is. But my first paid shift will be on opening night next week."

Harrison frowned. "You're training, and they're not paying you?"

"Dad, they don't have money yet. But I get paid cash after my first shift. They'll give me a bonus, I bet. I'm gonna do so awesome."

"Yeah, you will."

Although this dad didn't share his son's enthusiasm for unpaid training. Nor did he believe that the company couldn't afford to pay him yet.

"Well, I'm glad to hear you got the job," Harrison quickly added. "But don't let it get in the way of school, okay?"

"Of course!" Justin brought the phone closer to his face. "Damn, Dad, what are those dark circles under your eyes? Were you out late on a date?"

Busted. "Uh, yeah."

Justin arched an eyebrow. "Lazlo?"

"Yes." A familiar warmth spread through Harrison's chest. Just hearing the demon's name was...lovely.

"When am I meeting my new daddy?"

*I promise the novelty of me being a demon will wear off soon.*

"It's not that serious," Harrison mumbled. Voicing the sentence too loudly felt wrong, although he couldn't quite place why. "Look, I should let you go. I'll call you after supper, okay?"

"Okay. Work hard! Love you!"

"Love you too."

Harrison put his phone away and placed his goggles and mask back on his face. Nothing left between him, his circular saw, and a frame he should have finished building twenty minutes ago.

But he couldn't bring himself to start working. All he could think about was Lazlo.

Lazlo thought Harrison would lose interest soon enough. Gary assumed Harrison was just looking for sex. Justin wanted his father to get a boyfriend so said father would bother his son less.

It was hard to figure out what Harrison himself wanted when his whole life had been about meeting other people's expectations. All he knew was that he liked Lazlo. And the demon's penchant for trash. Lazlo had gone from giving others pleasure to finding his own pleasure.

There was a lot of courage in taking the path that allowed someone to live their most authentic life. Sometimes it had its pits (like losing the love of one's homophobic father), but the journey would ultimately reap such rich, rewarding benefits.

Wouldn't it?

Harrison was on his own path now. And while he didn't know what he wanted to see at the end of his journey, he wanted to join Lazlo while their paths were entwined.

Was that wrong?

No sooner had the thought crossed his mind did Harrison find his phone in his hand. Carefully, he opened the messages between him and Lazlo. There weren't many, but every line from Lazlo shaped itself in Harrison's heart as poetry.

He liked Lazlo. That was all.

Before he lost the courage, he messaged the demon.

*I miss you already. When can I see you this week?*

# CHAPTER 8

"*S*o your son got a job?"

Sauce dribbled down Lazlo's chin as he asked the question. A tentacle wiped his face with a napkin, but it didn't quite get everything. Harrison's chest tightened as he focused on the speck of plum sauce.

They were inside another sports bar. A quiet one, fortunately. Neither of Alberta's NHL teams were playing a game tonight, which meant only a few people were scattered across the dim vicinity.

"Yeah, it's a new bar called Mustard Point."

"Mustard? Not Muster?"

Harrison chuckled. "That's what I said too. Some cowboy thing. Nothing out of the ordinary for the city."

Lazlo licked his lower lip. "I don't mind mustard too much, I guess. It can be kind of spicy. But sometimes it just tastes like metal to me."

"Does it?"

"Say, you got any photos of your kid?"

For some reason, the question made Harrison's heart flutter. But he tried his best to be nonchalant as he opened the gallery on his phone. He didn't have many recent ones. Somewhere along the way, Justin stopped wanting to pose if it was his dad holding the camera.

Harrison picked a photo of Justin at Christmas. They had gone to a diner that happily served people who didn't want to cook for the holidays. Harrison had managed to snap a shot of Justin downing his favorite peppermint milkshake. It was one of the few photos from the last couple of years that had a clear view of his son's face.

Lazlo whistled as he took the phone with a tentacle. "It's hard to believe someone like you has an eighteen-year-old."

"I can't believe it myself some days." Harrison ran his hand through his hair. "His mom and I were really young when she got pregnant. We hadn't planned on him, but…"

But they had had him. And he had tried to make his family work as long as he could.

It was still a miracle that Harrison had been the one to raise Justin, considering everything. His ex had only returned to Calgary to visit their son twice in the last ten years. Never had Justin been invited to her house.

"Wow, he's got your eyes, doesn't he?" Lazlo held the phone with his hand now, going back and forth between looking at the screen and looking at Harrison. "Warm, soft, trusting. He must be gentle like you."

Harrison bit his lip, acutely aware of the heat in his cheeks. Did Lazlo have such nice thoughts about him?

And…did other people think of Justin as trusting? The conversation from the other day echoed in the back of Harrison's brain. Justin had been pretty willing to receive training without payment and clearly believed his new bosses had no money.

Was that the truth? Or were the folks behind Mustard Point taking advantage of a teenager who had barely dipped his toes into the adult world?

Harrison took his phone back and silently reminded himself that Justin didn't want him to interfere with his business. That his son wanted him to get busy with adult things and leave him alone.

Sigh.

Well, he could focus on his date, he supposed. It did help that said date was an attractive, trash-loving, tentacle-having demon.

The spot on Lazlo's chin continued to capture Harrison's attention. He clearly needed some assistance with it. And, well, okay, maybe the human was looking for an excuse to touch him.

He reached over the high top and wiped the spot for Lazlo with his thumb, allowing his forefinger to linger under the demon's soft chin. To the human's delight, Lazlo's face grew pink, and a bashful smile curled in the corner of his mouth.

Did Lazlo know how much his eyes—and the gems on his body—sparkled when he blushed?

Harrison grinned as he wiped his thumb on his napkin. "Sorry. It was bothering me."

*Please make a mess again.*

"No, no. I should be thanking you." Lazlo fussed with his ponytail. "We're almost out of wings. Do you wanna order more food?"

Harrison glanced at his plate. A stack of bones and a pool of barbecue sauce were all that remained of the platter of wings and French fries the pair had ordered for dinner. The beer pitcher next to them had run low as well.

"I'm not hungry," Harrison said. "But I'm also not eager to end our date yet. Unless you wanna call it a night."

Lazlo shook his head. His tentacles swayed in the same motion. "I'd rather hang out with you. What should we do?"

Good question.

Anxiety bore a hundred holes into Harrison's heart as he considered the possibilities. *Consider* was perhaps a bit of a generous word. It was more like he stared into a white space in his mind and waited for the answer to appear.

If he were a more interesting person, it wouldn't be difficult to propose an activity.

"I don't know," Harrison finally confessed. "There's a lot I don't know, really."

Lazlo chuckled. "Yeah, I get that. I'm the same way. When I'm not digging through trash or working, I'm at a loss. The human world is so big outside of the bedroom, you know? So much to learn, but I don't know the basics of anything."

Harrison tipped his head to the side. "What do you want to learn? I can help. I promise I won't make fun of you for anything. It's not like you should be expected to know everything as soon as you arrive in a new world."

"Yeah?" Lazlo smiled and gestured across the room with a particularly long tentacle. "What about those things? They have sticks, but you aren't supposed to jam them down the holes? I got yelled at once for doing that. What kind of game is it?"

Harrison looked over his shoulder. The billiard tables practically glowed as he realized they had found their new activity.

He hopped off the stool and reached for his wallet. "Don't worry. The game will make more sense once I'm done giving you a lesson."

Lazlo's ensuing intrigued expression swept away all the anxiety inside the human.

After renting the colorful balls from the bar, Harrison guided Lazlo a billiard table. He promptly grabbed the rack and began placing the balls inside the triangle. Though it had been years since Harrison had last played, setting up the game still felt familiar and fresh in his memories.

Lazlo ducked under the table briefly. He re-emerged with a scowl on his face. "Only gum down there. Why don't humans stick more exciting trash under tables?"

"Physics, probably." Harrison grinned and pointed to the table. "So, the variation we're going to play is eight-ball. This is probably the most common game people think of when it comes to billiards. I played it a lot with my buddies back when I was posing as straight and we wanted a night without our girlfriends or wives."

He paused during his explanation, recalling a few embarrassing vignettes of his past. All he could do was laugh. It was so long ago. Back when he assumed all he could do was suffocate every second he lived.

Now...he was breathing. Really breathing.

Lazlo scoffed. "You're telling me a game with long sticks and a bunch of balls is for the boys and enbies only?"

"Eh, more like pool has an odd 'straight men only' vibe to it. Especially in a sports bar." Harrison handed Lazlo a cue stick and picked up one for himself. "But that's okay. We're gay, and we're going to play."

"You're fucking right we are!"

Warmth spread through Harrison's chest as he met Lazlo's fired up expression. Though he had been out of the closet for a decade, there still hadn't been many occasions where he voiced his sexuality aloud. Fewer times where he empowered himself because of it. And there had never been an instance where his declarations were met with an approving cheer.

Until now.

Lazlo held the cue stick with his tentacles. "Which hole do I put this in?"

Ah, yes. There was going to have to be a very detailed explanation. But that was okay. Harrison liked teaching. And, of course, he liked every second he spent with Lazlo.

"Hold it with your hands, okay?" Harrison placed the cue ball along the break line. "And here, rub this chalk along the tip. Makes it easier to nail those shots. I'll show you."

Lazlo rested a few fingers on his cheek. "Oh, we're rubbing our tips to do some nailing now, are we?"

A ribbon of arousal escaped Harrison with his laughter as he finished his demonstration. "We're only just getting started. Wait until you see how we hold the shafts."

Was billiards always this stimulating? It had been stifling before, although the circumstances weren't very different. Felt tables, bellies full of beer and wings, hockey in the background. All that was different about now was Lazlo.

Harrison drank in the gem-covered demon as he removed the rack, briefly wondering if Lazlo made other people so…eager. There had never been a time in the human's life where he felt comfortable enough to flirt, let alone swap sexual innuendo.

"I'll let you break the rack," Harrison said.

A scowl crossed Lazlo's face. "Why do they hide the balls behind the bar if I'm supposed to break them?"

"No, no." Harrison chuckled. "Sorry. That's just a technical term. What it means is that you're going to use your cue stick to hit the white ball in the same direction as the other balls. Then you'll make them scatter across the table."

"Oh. That's a little less exciting."

Lazlo approached the table with his stick, but he still appeared to be at a loss for what to do. His tentacles also appeared to be on the limp side with the confusion.

"Like this." Harrison adjusted his posture, modeling how to hold the cue stick. "And then you slide the stick between your fingers like this."

Though Lazlo had his razor sharp focus on Harrison, nothing about his wrinkled expression suggested he understood what to do.

An idea occurred to Harrison. One that made him, well, more eager.

"Here."

Harrison set his stick down and approached from Lazlo behind. He gingerly wrapped one arm around the demon's thick body and used the other to make some adjustments.

"Hold the back of the stick at your hip and spread your legs—er, tentacles—like this." Harrison kept his voice low, trying not to get lost in how being so close to Lazlo made his head spin. "Bend low while you take your shot."

For a moment, the pair became one. A tentacle wrapped itself around Harrison's leg, ensuring he wouldn't leave Lazlo as his date focused on his shot. A pair of large, plump tentacles along the demon's back rubbed against Harrison's crotch while he settled into the right position. If it was accidental or intentional, it hardly mattered to the human.

He was in heaven, holding Lazlo and resting his hand on top of his. The heat of their bodies together was pure bliss. And the fact that Lazlo was taking his time to make his shot suggested the demon was fine with the current physical arrangement.

By now, a few guys had started playing a game at a table nearby. A couple of them looked at Harrison, but the shadows of the dimly lit bar masked the thoughts dancing in their eyes.

Regardless, the other group reminded Harrison of the most important thing—that he was holding Lazlo in public without a care who saw him. Even if someone tried to pick a fight with him for being affectionate in public, Harrison had enough salt and vinegar in him to fight back.

No more hiding. Ever.

Finally, Lazlo took his shot. The balls scattered in clumps that were on par for a beginner. Though none had sunk, enough had gathered along the rail to make the break valid.

"Good job," Harrison whispered in his ear.

Lazlo looked up. His golden eyes glowed with his sparkling smile, and his gravelly voice bordered on velvety as he asked, "Was that good?"

"Yes."

Neither of them seemed ready to move. For a few seconds, they stayed close like that, with their limbs entwined around each other and their mouths mere centimeters from kissing.

What did the jewels in Lazlo's mouth feel like? Or the suckers lingering under his tongue?

God, he had never wanted to kiss someone so much in his life.

When the tentacle untangled itself from Harrison's leg, he took that as a hint to step back. The immediate cold he felt as he did so lingered while he took his first shot.

Harrison gestured to one of the table's pockets. "Okay, since I sunk a striped ball, it's my intention to sink only stripes now until we get to the eight ball. That one should be saved for last, even though you're solids."

"What do we have against the eight ball?"

"Nothing." Harrison applied more chalk to his cue stick and shot the other group a look. They didn't seem to be paying much attention to them. Good. "That's just how the game goes. So, I'm going to take another shot. I keep shooting until I miss sinking one of my balls."

Lazlo's lips quirked with amusement, but he didn't say anything. He merely watched Harrison as if he were the most interesting human to wander the world. Or perhaps that was just how Harrison felt as he made his second shot, determined to impress his date with his skills.

Said skills, unfortunately, proved to be rusty. He missed.

"Okay." Harrison rubbed the back of his fiery neck, trying

to play it cool. "That was a foul. It's your turn now. You can aim for any of the solid colored balls."

"All right!" Lazlo picked up his stick, fumbled with it for a few moments, then glanced at Harrison. "Can you show me how I'm supposed to hold it again?"

Show him again? Like hold him again?

The eager human was not going to say no to that. And—maybe it was the beer talking, the decades of repressed feelings, or just the fact that he wanted to—but he decided to up his flirting game.

He ambled behind Lazlo and wrapped his arm around him, once again using the other arm to adjust his date's posture. His hand lingered on the demon's soft stomach as he brought his lips close to Lazlo's ear.

"But I'm going to have to charge you if you're going to keep needing such special guidance." Harrison's voice was low, gruff, and dripping with suggestive desires. He could hardly believe it was *him* talking like that.

"Oh, are you?"

Lazlo turned enough to meet Harrison's eyes. The smirk on his lovely lips and the softness of his question was a lethal combo. All the blood in Harrison's body rushed to his groin, and there was no way Lazlo didn't notice how much the human wanted him.

"A kiss per lesson would probably suffice," Harrison remarked, on the verge of stealing the kiss for himself. Or simply dropping to his knees and begging Lazlo to choke him.

Wait. Was *that* something he wanted?

Before Harrison could think too hard about his desires, one of Lazlo's tentacles grabbed him by the collar and brought their lips together, forcing every thought inside him to disappear.

Harrison had had his share of kisses, but never one with someone he actually wanted. Never had his entire body tingled with delight and need until this very moment. The kiss was light and soft, but Harrison's lips got a hint of the smooth jewels hiding in the demon's mouth and the promise of a tongue that had the power to shatter the human's world. One tentacle wrapped around Harrison's neck, prolonging the kiss and heightening every sensation pummeling through him.

It had never been this right to be so close to someone before.

A few, too short moments later, Lazlo broke the kiss. But he stayed close. The way he swiped his tongue along his lip seemed to be asking if that was a sufficient payment. God, Harrison wanted to immediately taste him again. Harder. Longer. Deeper.

Harrison glanced at the other group. Their eyes were turned to the pair. His spine stiffened as he braced himself for nasty comments or homophobic gestures. They had definitely seen him smooching Lazlo. Obviously, they had no idea that Lazlo was a demon. In their eyes, it had been two human men kissing.

Surprisingly, a couple of them gave him a thumbs up. The group returned to their own game.

A grin broke across Harrison's face as relief washed over him. Being his true self felt so *wonderful*. As good as kissing Lazlo.

Would he have these feelings with anyone else? He wanted to think so, but it was also difficult to deny that the pull he felt toward was Lazlo was strong. Even if they didn't kiss again, Harrison would never be able to forget that moment.

As soon as that realization hit him, he knew he'd never miss another chance to take his shot with Lazlo. For as long as Lazlo wanted him around, Harrison Hamilton would be there.

He turned his attention back to Lazlo and held him tighter as he guided him during the next shot.

And when it was Lazlo's turn again, the demon coyly asked for another lesson, sending a flare of hope through the human. The rest of the game passed with a lot of "lessons" that needed "payment." Every kiss was better than the last.

Lazlo clearly wanted Harrison. In what way, though, the human didn't know.

But he couldn't wait to find out.

# CHAPTER 9

*H*arrison checked his phone as soon as he woke up. Finally. The next date had arrived.

Lazlo and Harrison had gone on a few more dates (and shared a few more delicious kisses) over the past month since the memorable pool game, but it had been close to a week since the human had seen the demon. The demon had apparently been busy with his work for the city.

Each day without seeing Lazlo felt like a year, but it was manageable thanks to the demon texting him pictures frequently of interesting trash he found. Harrison, lacking trash pictures, sent him snapshots of the hamsters. Tiger and Leopard were huge hits in the demon's heart.

The pair had fallen into a cute routine as well. Every morning, Lazlo would call Harrison while he waited for the train. The conversations would be short, but hearing Lazlo's voice for a few minutes stirred awake every molecule inside the human. The demon always asked about Harrison's plans for the day and inquired about how Justin was doing at his university and job—questions Harrison didn't always have an answer for since his son didn't answer calls or texts much lately.

Lazlo was due to call soon. Harrison couldn't wait. This morning's call would be about going over their plans for that night. It was going to be a very special date. The pair were supposed to go to a hockey game with a secret trip to the stadium's bins afterward. It was going to be an evening full of noise, drunks, and the fear of breaking one's neck since they were going to sit in the nosebleeds.

But it was going to be an evening with Lazlo. That was all Harrison cared about.

He sent a message to Lazlo, and then he attempted video calling Justin. As it was a Saturday, his son didn't have any classes. But it was likely he was still sleeping in. Maybe after a late night at work. And possibly a later night of drinking. Youths always found energy to party after work, a character-istic Harrison sometimes envied when he listened to his younger coworkers.

The video call rang nearly a dozen times. No answer. Not even a glimpse of a groggy teenager and a faint promise to call back later.

Well. Hopefully, everything was all right. Maybe Justin was just busy. And his son had made it clear he didn't need his dad anymore.

Harrison licked his teeth, detecting a hint of rust.

While he grabbed himself a glass of water and debated stepping out for a smoke, his phone rang. It wasn't Justin returning the call, but his lips quirked with delight when he saw Lazlo's name on his screen.

Harrison answered before the second ring, a bright grin on his face and his chest tightening with glee. Warmth rushed through him, imagining how cuddled up the two would have to sit to keep Lazlo's tentacles from touching someone else. Perhaps all of Lazlo's tentacles would have to

75

wrap around the human to keep him from invading someone else's space.

"Hey," Harrison said, with all the eloquence a horny man was able to possess.

"Hey," Lazlo replied. "Uh, sorry, but I'm going to have to cancel our date tonight."

Harrison circled around the kitchen island with his water in one hand and his phone in the other. Oof. Those words had knocked the sun out of the sky.

Was this the end of his romance with the demon? Had Lazlo grown bored with Harrison? Was he worried that Harrison was going to push him for something he didn't want? Had there been too many kisses during their last date?

Great. Now Harrison was going to be riddled with anxiety all day. And all month. Maybe all of forever.

"You don't have to apologize," Harrison replied, trying to keep the edge out of his voice. "And you're doing a good job of sounding like a stereotypical Canadian."

"Thanks, eh."

A weak laugh swirled in Harrison's ear. Now that he thought about it, Lazlo sounded like he had swallowed a bunch of rocks. There was also a distinct lack of background noise that was usually prominent at the train station.

"Are you okay?" Harrison stopped his pacing. "What's going on?"

"Don't worry about it. I'll figure it out."

Harrison leaned against the island and set down his water. "What is it? Can't I help you?"

A long silence passed between them. All Harrison could hear was a faint breath, brimming with hesitation.

Finally, Lazlo spoke again. "It's demon stuff, I guess. Demons don't naturally live here, right?"

"Uh-huh?" Not that the human knew. Before Lazlo, Harrison had had no idea of the existence of actual demons.

"So demons need to renew their energy to keep living here."

Where was this conversation heading? Harrison's heart sank to his stomach.

Lazlo cleared his throat. "Let's just say I'm sick."

Sick? Why didn't he just say so right away?

"I can bring you anything you need." Harrison scratched the back of his head. "What are your symptoms? There has to be something that can help you. Juice? Crackers? Medicine?"

"Don't worry about it, eh?" Lazlo's words rolled out of him slowly, with an uncharacteristic uneasiness. "As much as I brag about being a trash demon, I'm a pleasure demon at my core. There's only one way for me to keep getting energy. So I'm trying to figure out how to get that energy. But it's difficult."

Another silence fell between them. Harrison concentrated on the sound of Lazlo's labored breath, his veins twisting with desperation to figure out what he could do to help. If the demon couldn't find the energy he needed, then he couldn't stay in this world. And Harrison wasn't ready to stop seeing Lazlo.

What sort of energy did a pleasure demon require—

"Sex?"

The word tumbled out of Harrison's mouth before it could register properly in his brain. But as soon as those three little letters echoed through his ear, his world came to a halt.

The answer had to be something sexual. Sex bored Lazlo, but he needed the energy from it to survive in this realm. It wasn't like the demon couldn't easily find someone to bed. Lazlo's handsome human disguise could woo humans by the dozen. And there was a very willing participant on the phone call who'd bang him, tentacles and all.

Heat flashed through Harrison. Could he offer himself

like that? His first time ever with a man? To help the demon get better?

While his heart was uncertain, his rigid cock had a different response.

Harrison palmed himself over his pajama pants, trying to get his body to calm down. But those urgent touches also sent a warped thrill through him.

Finally, Lazlo spoke again. "Yeah. Sex. Specifically, I get power by making someone orgasm."

A hundred vignettes, all of them with Harrison on the receiving end of Lazlo's ministrations, passed through the human. Oh, how he wanted to jump in his truck and speed to Lazlo's side!

But the resignation in Lazlo's voice also killed that desire to offer his body.

Harrison took a long drink of cold water, trying harder to make himself, well, less hard. "And you don't want to?"

"It's not that I don't want to, but..." Lazlo sighed. "Sorry. Maybe I should have told you earlier so all of this would be less confusing. I'm bored with *casual* sex, you get it? Only banging to fulfill my physical needs hollowed me out inside. For thousands of years, I've banged everything that's wanted to be serviced by me, but it always ends after the orgasm. They all forget about my existence."

As Lazlo opened up, Harrison pressed the phone closer to his ear, now wishing he was at the demon's side for a different reason. His heart fractured, picturing the pain etched in Lazlo's lovely face. The demon was always full of smiles and mischief.

"And you became a trash demon to find a new kind of pleasure, right?" Harrison asked.

"Yeah. It was suggested to me. So far, I've been enjoying all the fine dumpsters, greasy alleys, and condemned houses this city has to offer. But it's not sustaining me, you know?"

Harrison bit his lower lip, trying to think of a solution. One that wasn't just *fuck the closest willing person and do what you need to keep seeing me*. That would be selfish.

And how could so many people (and other creatures) get to know a cheery, playful, wonderful demon like Lazlo and forget him after sex? That seemed impossible.

By now, a small part of Harrison worried if *he* would lose interest in Lazlo after bedding him. As much as he wanted to fuck the demon, he didn't want to risk losing what they had going on. Offering himself seemed to be off the table.

Harrison sucked in a sharp breath and attempted to push his personal desires away. "What happens if you don't make someone orgasm soon?"

"Oh, I'll die."

What?!

"Ah, don't freak out, Hamtaro!" Lazlo chuckled. "I'll get reborn. I've had some dry spells in my past."

Was…was that supposed to be comforting? Harrison certainly wasn't comforted.

He began circling around his kitchen island, gripping his phone. "Pretty sure I'm allowed to freak out a little there, eh, don't you think? I don't want anything bad to happen to you. Ever."

"Don't say things you don't mea—"

"I mean it."

Harrison paused, taking in the shakiness of his fingers and the way his mouth suddenly tasted like metal. These sensations weren't new to him. He had experienced this kind of anxiety—the way his heart pumped as much blood as it could to his brain while he scrambled for ideas—multiple times over the years. From finding out he had gotten his girlfriend pregnant to Justin's first bender fender a few months ago, Harrison had fine-tuned his panic process to an art.

What was new was the target of his worries. He never

worried this much about anyone who wasn't close to him. For years, the only person close enough to merit such thought had been Justin.

Yet here Harrison was, acutely aware that he'd later only consume cigarettes for breakfast because he didn't want Lazlo to suffer and didn't have a solution.

He pinched the bridge of his nose. No, that wasn't true. There was one clear solution. A risky one, if what Lazlo said earlier was true.

"Use me." Harrison pumped his words with confidence, though his lips trembled. "Let me take care of you. If there's nothing I can do for you but *that*, then use me."

There. It was out in the open. The possible ending of his brief ride with Lazlo. The demon would get his needed energy, and the human...

Well, he didn't know what would happen to him. That unknown possibilities terrified him immensely.

But letting something bad happen to Lazlo would be a thousand times worse than whatever might happen to Harrison.

"No." The demon's voice had grown rougher than ever, like a tentacle was squeezing his neck. "Not you. I can't chance you not wanting to see me anymore."

A protest danced on Harrison's tongue, but he couldn't immediately set it free. Not when his brain had stopped and connected the dots.

Lazlo wanted to keep dating him.

Heat exploded through Harrison as the realization set in that this was about more than dating. It wouldn't be hard to find other humans to date. MapleMance with rife with potential matches.

No. Lazlo had come to care for him. It wasn't just Harrison spending nights listening to Nickelback and getting the strings of his heart tugged when a yearning lyric resonated with him.

"Sorry," Lazlo quickly added. "I mean—"

"Let's have a date."

Harrison's proposition had to be released before he lost the nerve. The demon he adored needed help. And he absolutely would help.

The tremor in Harrison's lips and fingers traveled through his entire body as he continued talking. "We don't have to go to the hockey game. Let's just go for a drive out of the city and see what happens. You, me, some mountains. Alone. I also don't want to stop seeing you. At any cost."

What felt like an eternity passed before Lazlo finally responded. "Okay. Come pick me up at noon. But I won't blame you if you change your mind."

After ending the call, Harrison stepped outside for a smoke, but he couldn't light the cigarette from the tumultuous way his hands shook.

What happened next would change his life. In what way, he couldn't predict. Nothing about his life had ever been predicted correctly.

But after several weeks of digging through trash with Lazlo, being teased by the suckers under the demon's tongue whenever they kissed, getting heart emojis every time he sent a picture of his hamsters, and feeling like the real him for the first time ever, Harrison knew which direction he hoped life would take him.

# CHAPTER 10

*W*ith a clear cerulean sky and the warm sun shining down on them, the pair headed north to Banff. Though it was early April, there would still be plenty of snow on the ground and mountains to admire, but the roads would be clear of ice.

Harrison glanced at his quiet date, who had his eyes glued to the passing scenery. Neither of them had said anything for the last forty minutes or so.

When he had picked up Lazlo earlier, all it had taken was a single look to know that the demon was sick. Lazlo's vibrant red hair had lost its luster, his tentacles had gone limp, and the gems on his skin were cloudy. Perhaps most concerning, the demon had worn a flannel shirt with only minimal tearing for his appendages. His black leggings and slides were in perfect condition.

Had the demon dressed up to make up for how ill he appeared? Or did he want to look extra nice for what might potentially be their last date?

"We're getting close to a lake that has a good hiking trail," Harrison said, unable to deal with the silence any longer. "We

MATCH WITH THE DEMON

should stop and look around the picnic areas. You might enjoy looking through the trash there."

"Yeah, I guess that would be fine."

Ugh. Lazlo sounded so weak and incredibly unenthused. He really needed help.

They still hadn't agreed to actually let Lazlo do whatever he needed to do with Harrison. The conversation was waiting to happen, but neither of them had approached the subject. In all fairness, Harrison also wanted to have one more memorable date with Lazlo before...

Before whatever came next.

Snow-kissed trees began to frame the long, empty road. Once they passed through the toll gate and the natural splendor of Alberta's beauty came into full view, it was a wonder there were no other vehicles around. Hints of green peeked through the sea of giant larch trees, and chunks of white ice swam in the turquoise lakes.

Harrison kicked himself for nearly missing the chance to surround himself in the ephemeral moment between winter and spring. Immediately, he wanted to pull over and start snapping pictures—of the lakes, the mountains, Lazlo's bright smile as he rummaged through the bear-resistant bins.

His heart tied into a knot as he peered at the glum figure in the passenger seat. There had yet to be a single trace of a grin to cross Lazlo's lovely face during their outing.

"We don't have to drag this out." Harrison cleared his throat and tried to keep his eyes on the road. Tried not to let the terror welling within him keep him from making any mistakes. "You need energy, and I can help."

Something soft brushed against his shoulder. A tentacle. Harrison grabbed it gently and let his fingers curl around the appendage. The suckers had grown hard, less alive.

"I'm not scared or anything," Harrison mumbled, once more tasting a sheet of metal in his mouth. "Let me help you."

"No." Lazlo pulled away from him. "You know I like hanging out with you, right?"

Harrison pressed his lips together and began to drive slower. It was getting difficult to focus. All he wanted to do was gaze at Lazlo and commit every gem to memory. Do everything he could to ensure himself he wouldn't forget the demon if they became intimate.

Lazlo drummed a few fingers along the window. "I won't lie to you. Ever since I watched you guzzle a mug of beer like you had just returned from the belly of a fire demon, I've wanted to know what you look like when you orgasm."

An uncomfortable cocktail of heat and anxiety washed through the human as he listened. His whole life, he had wanted to hear a man tell him that he was desirable. To fall into bed with someone who saw the real Harrison Hamilton and use his mouth to promise a beautiful new beginning.

Now that the precious words were rippling in his ears, they sounded like the start of an ending.

"And I've seen the way you look at me. Really look." Lazlo sighed. "I kept waiting for you to get bored with dating a demon. You didn't."

"How could I?" Carefully, Harrison removed his jacket. It had grown too warm in the vehicle for layers. "Not when the demon is you."

A weak chortle filled the space between them. "You always know what to say. And I like that henley you're wearing. Your collarbone always looks so inviting."

Inviting. Why wasn't Harrison more thrilled with such a compliment?

"I wish I liked you less." Lazlo's words had a tremble to them. "I wish it was easy for me to take you up on your generous offer with all your bravery. Everything hurts inside right now. A lot."

Somehow, Harrison kept driving. What he really wanted

to do, though, was pull the demon into his embrace. Hug Lazlo and promise him everything would be fine.

But he didn't know. He had never had an honest romance with a human. The least he could do now was be truthful with the demon he had fallen for.

"Actually, I'm scared," Harrison confessed. "I don't know what's going to happen. But I want to help you."

Slowly, a tentacle made its way back to Harrison's lap. So little heat radiated from the crimson beauty.

"Then I won't do anything more than this," Lazlo whimpered. "I guess I should get over myself and look for a random horny person. Use someone without a care. Something always happens after sex to make me disappear from my partner. When I come back, they can't see me. The same would be true for you, and I just can't—"

Enough.

Harrison pulled over to the side of the road and threw the truck in park, leaving the ignition running to ward off wildlife.

He awkwardly unbuckled himself and turned toward Lazlo. Confusion contorted the edges of the demon's unique features. Lazlo's golden eyes were covered in shadows that Harrison was determined to dissipate.

"I hope I don't forget you." Harrison ran his finger down the rigid tentacle on his lap. "Ever since our first date, I haven't been able to stop thinking about you."

Lazlo sat up straight and unbuckled his own seatbelt. His mouth began to move, but Harrison barreled on.

"I also don't want you dying because you can't bring yourself to bone a random stranger." Harrison gave Lazlo's tentacle a gentle squeeze. "Your comfort matters more than me continuing to go on dates with probably the most amazing guy in all the realms, and if you're comfortable with me, then let me help you. I want to take this risk."

"Harrison..."

Something about Lazlo shifted. The shadows clinging to his visage disappeared. A dim glow brought his eyes back to life. All the heat in the vehicle rose to new, almost smothering levels as his tentacle slipped away from Harrison's grasp and began rubbing against his jeans.

Everything was so scary.

And also exciting.

Harrison leaned forward and pressed his lips lightly to Lazlo's dry mouth. Several tentacles crawled up his arms and around his neck. There was still enough slack for Harrison to escape—not that he wanted to. Wrapped in Lazlo's appendages, the terror in his chest remained, but he couldn't taste a hint of metal. All he could taste was his desire for the demon.

Right now, he was exactly where he wanted to be. And his growing erection agreed with him.

As he leaned back, he murmured, "Use me. Take everything you need."

The human's hands went for his belt, but a couple of tentacles stopped him. Harrison chewed on his lower lip and watched the small tentacles free his cock.

No sooner had the half-hard member tasted air did one tentacle begin to stroke him. Those first waves of pleasure pulsed through Harrison like lightning, causing the hair on the back of his neck to stiffen.

*Fuck.*

Everything was happening so fast, but Harrison had surrendered himself to Lazlo. With expert finesse, the demon ensured all the blood in Harrison's body went to his cock. The suckers began to wiggle with newfound life as the tentacle wrapped itself around his length.

A groan escaped Harrison. As scared as he was of what might happen after, he was more than ready to be pleased by

Lazlo. Especially now that a familiar, mischievous smirk had returned to his face.

"If I had known you were hiding such a large beast in your pants, I might have taken you sooner," Lazlo cooed. His voice had turned into pure silk, so soft and smooth. "Do you see how pink your cheeks are now in the mirror? You're that way because of me."

Harrison glanced in the rearview mirror, but he couldn't focus on himself at all. While the tentacles around his arms squeezed him, the appendage hugging his neck traveled toward his mouth. The tip teased the corner of his mouth, and Harrison wanted nothing more than to suck it—to have as much of Lazlo in him as possible.

Lazlo's smirk widened as he continued jerking off Harrison. Every movement was divine. With each passing second, the human experienced new heights of pleasure.

"You look so gorgeous, babe," Lazlo purred. "Promise me you're going to give me every drop of your cum. I really need it. I really need you."

"Yes." Another groan rolled out of Harrison. It had grown so hot, everything was almost unbearable. But he definitely didn't want it to stop. "You can have all of me."

"I can, can't I?"

Relief swept through Harrison as Lazlo's tentacle slipped between his lips. Pure bliss shuddered through him as his tongue collided against the soft, warm tentacle. It was difficult to describe the stark sensation of the suckers clinging to him while Lazlo's smooth gems rubbed against the top of his mouth.

*More. Go deeper in me.*

To his disappointment, Lazlo pulled away from his mouth. All of the demon's attention had turned to Harrison's cock.

"Look at the mess you're already making down there."

Lazlo chuckled. "From the way you're shaking, you're going to come soon, aren't you?"

That was...a very fair assessment. All the excitement of Harrison's first time with someone else in years plus Lazlo's expert skills added up to a great need to relieve himself as soon as possible.

The tentacle that had been in Harrison's mouth wandered to Lazlo's ruby lips. Watching the demon suck himself made Harrison forget about everything except that he needed to taste Lazlo again.

"Come here." Harrison gently broke from a tentacle holding his arm and grabbed his lover by the collar of his shirt, tugging him close. "Kiss me."

The pair had shared many teasing kisses, but those all became distant memories as the demon leaned in and gave the human exactly what he wanted. Lazlo's tongue glided against Harrison's while they locked lips, overloading the human with a variety of textures from the wet organ, the eager suckers, and the occasional bump of the gems. Harrison could hardly keep up with the demon's enthusiasm.

Soon, the tentacle that had been in their mouths replaced the one pleasuring Harrison's cock. On multiple fronts, the human was treated to a feast of writhing suckers and slick ministrations.

Everything was so hot, so wet, so perfect. Harrison couldn't help moaning directly into Lazlo's mouth as his climax gushed out of him. The pleased noise from Lazlo as his appendages became covered in Harrison's cum was the icing to the cake.

Harrison shut his eyes for a moment, shaking from how wonderful he felt. That had been the best orgasm of his life. And it wasn't because it had been a man or a demon getting him off.

It was because it had been *Lazlo* touching him. No one else was ever going to make him feel that blissed.

When Harrison opened his eyes, delight swept through him. Already, Lazlo had a healthy glow to him again. His hair and tentacles had their beautiful luster to them again, and the gems along his body sparkled like his interested eyes.

From the demon's intense, pointed look, it was obvious Lazlo wasn't done having fun with Harrison.

Harrison broke into a bright smile and pulled him into another kiss. He wrapped his arms around Lazlo's torso, ensuring his lover didn't leave him. Several of the tentacles remained entwined protectively around Harrison. For several moments, they stayed in each other's embrace, sharing long, heated kisses.

As Harrison's dick began to grow to life again, he broke from the kiss, just long enough to ask an important question.

"We're quite a ways from home, but I'm absolutely not risking a bear or moose crashing in on us. Should we go find a hotel?"

"Fuck, ye—"

The precious moment shattered with a loud ring.

Crap. It was Harrison's phone. Did he actually have service up here? Seriously? What scammers were trying to interrupt the most important afternoon of his life?

"Ignore it," Harrison grunted. "Actually, no. Let me decline it so we can get the GPS and find—"

One of the tentacles held up Harrison's phone. Lazlo had already put some space between the pair. The shadows had returned to his face, and his mouth curved downward in a way that practically broke Harrison's heart.

Whoever was calling would just have to wait. He had to kiss his demon boyfriend until he cheered up.

Wait.

That was Justin's name on the screen. And it wasn't a

video call. It was a regular call, which was something his son *never* did.

"Shit. I'm sorry." Harrison grabbed the phone. "It shouldn't be more than a second. Justin will leave me alone once he knows I'm on a date."

The reassurance appeared to do little for Lazlo. At once, all the warm tentacles left Harrison's body.

Harrison tucked his dick back in his boxers and jeans as he answered the call. "Hey, buddy, sorry, but I'm out with Lazlo, and—"

"Oh my God, Dad, I think I'm going to have a complete breakdown. Where are you?"

The pain entrenched in Justin's words froze everything inside Harrison. His son's voice lacked its usual cheekiness, and Justin wasn't prone to hyperbole about his bad situations.

Something was seriously wrong with him.

Acidic, metallic bile rose up Harrison's throat. "What's going on?"

"What isn't wrong?" Justin sobbed. "I'm sorry. I got fired from Mustard Point, and they won't pay me, and everything's been really shitty for a while, and I don't know what to do."

Oh, no.

He couldn't just ignore Justin like this. But Lazlo…

Harrison glanced at the stony-faced demon next to him. Lazlo's lips quirked, but they never quite stretched into a smile.

"Turn the truck around and go see him," Lazlo whispered. "I'll be fine. Thanks for everything."

Everything tasted like rust as the finality of those words struck Harrison. He tried to protest, but before he could say anything, Lazlo disappeared in a cloud of red mist.

Fuck.

# CHAPTER 11

*U*nable to reach Lazlo after the magical disappearing act, Harrison decided to focus on Justin. Once he had taken care of his son, he would smooth things over with Lazlo.

They *were* going to see each other again. They absolutely would. Harrison wasn't going to forget about him. There was no way Lazlo would ever just become *trash*.

As Harrison shifted into Dad Mode, while choking down half a pack of cigarettes, he tried to brace himself for the storm that was about to happen. Justin had had more than his fair shares of bad days, but whatever was going on now was new. Usually, the father had to pry his son to open up about his inner feelings. For the eighteen-year-old to call him while crying…

Harrison wasn't sure if he was ready for this unexplored territory.

But he had to do it. He *wanted* to do it. His own father had never been there for him. Harrison would sure as shit always be there for Justin.

When he reached home—where Justin's car was already

parked in the driveway—Harrison allowed himself half of another cigarette and reminded himself that the two had survived this long together. Whatever was going on, the Hamiltons would get through it.

He left his jacket in the truck and headed inside. He found his son sitting on the living room floor, cleaning the hamster cages while the little floofs scampered around the carpet in their individual exercise balls.

"You're old enough to stress clean now, huh?" Harrison plopped onto the couch, trying to catch a glimpse of his son's face hiding behind his dark curls.

"I guess."

Harrison slowly slumped to the floor, despite knowing his back was going to yell at him later for sitting like a teenager. Instead of forcing Justin to spill the beans right away, he just watched his son clean. Justin's hands usually moved nimbly, but his gestures were slow and tight.

After a couple of minutes, Justin finally looked up. His cheeks were dirty, and the whites of his puffy eyes had turned pink. A part of Harrison shriveled to nothing as he took in the fragile expression.

Right now, it was his top priority to make his son smile again and feel okay.

"So, you got fired?" Harrison asked. "What for? And you said they're not paying you?"

Justin clenched his jaw. "Yeah. It happened yesterday. My bosses asked me to pick up more shifts this weekend, but I told them I couldn't work that much. I'm so behind on my essays, and I've got a lot of exams to study for. They told me they needed me to flexible and that I wasn't being a team player, so they told me to turn in my things and to forget seeing my check."

"Okay, well, don't worry about *that*, all right?" Harrison rubbed Justin's shoulder. A deep anger began to brew inside him, but he did his best to stay calm. "That's a bullshit reason to let you go, and regardless of why you got fired, they have to pay you. You know the hours you worked, right? We'll get it sorted."

"But it's not that easy." Justin sighed as he finished wiping down the empty cage. "I did so much for them off the clock. Like, I went to the bar between classes and signed some package deliveries for them while they were busy with other stuff. I just wanted to help, you know? But I don't even really know what I should be paid for."

By now, there was enough fire inside Harrison to drive him downtown and set the weasels ablaze. How dare these assholes with shit taste in business names take advantage of his son like that?

But he had to keep his cool. Justin probably wouldn't know how to bail him out of jail. And his son also didn't need another thing to stress over.

Right. Justin had alluded on the phone that there was more trouble than being fired from his lousy job.

"What else is going on?" Harrison picked up the bag of hamster waste and tied it together. With a silent prayer to his knees, he managed to rise to his feet.

"Ugh, did I say anything about that?"

Harrison disposed of the trash and returned to the living room. Once again, Justin had his attention solely on the cages and cleaning supplies. As much as Justin loved the hamsters, he never cleaned the cages with such focus. It was obvious he didn't want his dad to see his embarrassment.

"Has it really been that bad?" Harrison frowned and leaned against the entryway. "What's been going on?"

"I don't know. All my classes are hard, I guess." Justin kept his head low. "And it's been hard to focus on anything because I was doing so much work. But I was spending so much money on gas and late night meals that I didn't have any cash to do anything fun. Just drink cheap shit with my friends."

"No girls?"

"None." Justin added fresh bedding to the cages. "You remember Ashley Burton?"

"Uh, vaguely."

Truthfully, there had been a few too many girls in Justin's life for Harrison to remember all of them.

"She was my girlfriend in grade twelve." Justin looked up at him. "Uh, the third one. She has red hair."

Harrison nodded, still not entirely sure if he knew who his son was talking about. "What about her?"

"She transferred to my university this semester, and she's been telling all the other girls to stay away from me because I broke up with her while we were at a dinner party her parents were hosting. That I was really tacky and inconsiderate. But her family was such trash!"

Oh, *that* Ashley Burton. With more details coming into play, Harrison recalled his son coming home in a suit jacket too big for him and grumbling about what trash the Burtons were, but Justin never said what exactly happened.

"So are the university girls listening to Ashley?" Harrison arched an eyebrow. "Is that why your dating life is a bit dry right now?"

A loud, exasperated sigh shot out of Justin. Which answered that question.

Harrison joined Justin on the floor again and quietly helped him reassemble the cage. Once they put the hamsters back in their homes and washed up, Harrison pivoted to the only comfort he shared with his son—food.

"Should we order something?" Harrison rubbed Justin's shoulder. "What do you want to eat?"

"Doesn't matter. You pick."

Christ. Things really were serious if Justin didn't want to

choose the menu. And it wasn't like Harrison was necessarily hungry, either. Not when his child was falling apart.

"Want to keep talking about what's on your mind?" Harrison wandered to the kitchen and opened the fridge. There were a few beers in there, and Justin could stay the night if he wanted to get wasted with his old man. "Want a beverage?"

"Maybe a pop."

No alcohol? Harrison grabbed two colas and brought them to the living room. By now, Justin had curled up on the couch and had the hood of his sweatshirt covering as much of his face as possible. Despite knowing he was very much an adult, Justin resembled a pouting eight-year-old.

Harrison sat down next to him and set the colas on the coffee table. Then he pulled Justin into a tight hug.

"It's all gonna be okay, you know?" Harrison spoke gently, secretly relishing the warmth of the somber moment. "We're going to get things sorted with your work, we can get you caught up on your courses, and high school drama is only going to last so long. You broke up with Ashley because you weren't comfortable with her family for whatever reason, and you're the most easygoing kid I know. Whatever drama is going on at university will pass. You prioritized your comfort, which is a remarkably mature decision. Women are going to see that characteristic and flock to you."

The strings of Harrison's heart tugged at his organ as the past two months came to mind.

Justin sighed. "Will it really pass? I was thinking I should transfer."

"You can do that if you want." Harrison paused. "Why weren't you comfortable with her family? You never told me."

"Ugh. They were saying such homophobic nonsense at that dinner, and Ashley knew I had, well, that I had you. She didn't give me a heads up about her parents or stand up to them or anything. So I assumed she shared their views or was willing to tolerate them."

Oh.

"Sorry," Justin added. "I didn't want to tell you then, but I just don't wanna be with anyone who doesn't accept my family. The love of my life and her family both have to get along with you."

Harrison kept hugging him, amazed by what a wonderful kid he had. If Harrison had been true to his values back when he had been Justin's age, his life would have been dramatically different.

But he also wouldn't have had Justin.

And he wouldn't have met a certain… A certain…

"Thanks, Dad." Justin eased away, wiping his eyes. "I thought I could do my adult stuff all by myself and let you live your life. But university life is harder than I thought it would be."

"Let me live my life?" Harrison sat up straight. "Is that honestly why you were trying to keep to yourself?"

Justin removed his hood and ran his hand through his tousled curls. "Yeah, I told you that, didn't I?"

"Yes, but I thought—"

"I'm not ignorant. I know you gave up a lot to raise me. You deserve to have fun. Not worry over a mess like me forever."

A wide grin unfurled across Harrison's face. For the first time since Justin had moved out, he felt secure about his relationship with his son. The eighteen-year-old needed his dad, just like the almost forty-year-old needed his son.

"I'm always going to worry over you." Harrison chose his words carefully and tried not to tear up. "That's just how it's going to be. I want to always be in your life. For as long as you will let me while I breathe, I'll be there to help. You're my family."

Justin returned the smile. "Thanks. I love you."

"Love you too." Harrison ruffled Justin's hair. "When are you going to decide what we're eating for dinner? I'm getting hungry."

"Speaking of family and dinners…" Justin grabbed Harrison's phone and began browsing the food delivery app. "When are you going to have an awkward dinner where I can meet Lazlo?"

Lazlo.

A storm passed through Harrison as incredibly vivid memories of the afternoon returned. The way they had been tangled together, the erratic beat of his heart during the heated kisses, all the words that had been left unsaid.

Where was the forlorn demon who had disappeared in a crimson haze?

Harrison eyed his phone in Justin's hand, desperate to snatch it back and find Lazlo. His posture grew stiff as metal coated his tongue once more. What would he say if he managed to get a hold of him? How could he convince the vulnerable demon that he still wanted to see him?

More than see. He wanted to do everything with Lazlo—kiss him, fuck him, eat wings and drink beer together, visit dark alleys brimming with garbage.

"Come on." Justin nudged Harrison in the side, snapping him out of his fugue. "Just set up a dinner sometime. Next week?"

Harrison blinked. "You really want to meet Lazlo?"

"Uh, yeah." Justin's warm chuckle eased the knots in Harrison's shoulders. "You've never made a bad decision in your life, so I trust this guy you're in love with is just right for you. Let me meet my new daddy."

That wasn't true. There had been plenty of bad decisions

in the past. There was a bad decision made every time he lit a cigarette or read one of Gary's texts.

But Lazlo definitely wasn't one of them.

And as for the being in love part...

"Okay." Harrison took back his phone. "I'll make it happen. I want you to meet him. If I have it my way, Lazlo will be a part of our family for a very long time."

"Really?" Justin broke into a grin. "Awesome. I love to hear that."

Harrison swiped through the menu options. "You're taking too damn long to order food, so I'm getting us an extra large donair pizza. I've been wanting that for a while."

"Ooh, me too! Good choice."

When the first bite of spicy donair beef, sweet garlicky sauce, and slightly tangy mozzarella hit Harrison's tastebuds, everything came into focus. Resolution thrummed through him as he inhaled each delicious slice of pizza.

From now on, he was going to pursue everything he wanted.

# CHAPTER 12

*A*fter Justin left—much happier and more relaxed than earlier in the day—Harrison headed outside with his phone, keys, and cigarettes. He would call Lazlo first, of course. No texting. If he didn't answer, then the desperate human would hop in the truck and drive to his man's place.

It was important that Lazlo knew as soon as possible from Harrison's own lips that what had happened that afternoon wasn't a one-off. That this human was never, ever going to forget the short, sweet, funny, hot demon.

His stomach tightened as he called Lazlo. It had grown quite cold outside, and puffy clouds covered the night sky. No doubt a few trace reminders of winter would fall from the sky.

Harrison brought a cigarette to his lips and prayed that Lazlo was still somewhere in this realm, ready to enjoy a frustrating spring of snowflakes with the other residents of this city. With him, specifically.

As three rings passed—with Harrison fumbling to light

his smoke because his hands shook so much—the telltale taste of metal returned.

What if Lazlo *had* left? What if Harrison drove to his tent and found it empty?

Or...what if Lazlo just didn't want to see Harrison anymore?

Finally, after the fourth ring, a familiar gravelly voiced curled in his ear. "Harrison?"

"You answered!"

Harrison shoved the cigarette and lighter back in his pack. As if he could focus on anything else right now. He stepped back inside, determined to find his jacket. Now that he had heard Lazlo's voice, he had to see him immediately.

But the jacket wasn't on the coat rack. Had he left it in the living room?

"I can't believe you're calling me." Lazlo cleared his throat. "You, uh, know who this is, right?"

"Of course I do. *Lazlo.*"

Harrison weaved through the living room and kitchen in search of his jacket. No dice. He'd just have to get a different one from his bedroom.

"And...you meant to call me?"

"Yes." Harrison marched upstairs. "I'm sorry I didn't call you earlier, but I wanted to make sure I could devote all of my attention to you first. Where are you? Can I see you? Please let me see you."

A pause slipped between them. "You want to see me?"

"Yes!"

Harrison stopped in his bedroom and smacked his forehead, remembering that he had left his jacket in his truck. Ah, what a fool he was! He could have been on his way to Lazlo's one full minute ago.

But it was fine. Everything would be fine. He believed it,

now that the truth of his feelings encompassed every thought in his brain. All he needed to do was get Lazlo to believe him.

After a lifetime of hiding in the shadows and doubting every decision he made, confidence and ease flowed through his veins. There was no one in the world who could stop him but the demon.

"Those other people you fucked didn't love you like I do." Harrison broke into a wide smile, enjoying the fact the confession had jumped out of him with no restraints. "So let me see you as soon as possible and show you."

Another pause passed between them. Harrison clutched the keys in his fist, hopeful he'd soon be on his way to give Lazlo everything he deserved.

A quiet sigh filled the space. "You always know what to say, don't you? What should I do?"

"Let me come to you." Harrison laughed. "You can take that statement in any way you want."

Without missing a beat, Lazlo replied, "I'll come to you."

"Huh?"

A ruby haze rolled through Harrison's bedroom. When the mist disappeared, the human was delighted to find a demon smiling at him.

"You love me, eh?"

Lazlo's voice had morphed into pure silk once more, those soft notes starting a fire in Harrison's belly.

The human ended the call, his grin stretching to new lengths as he drank in the treasure before him. Lazlo was extra lovely in this moment. His hair and tentacles glowed a bright red, mixing with the golden glimmer emanating from his hungry eyes. The gems on his thick body sparkled as if they had just been polished.

Notably, Lazlo had arrived without any clothes. A sea of crimson jewels along his round stomach pointed to a slit between his two larger tentacles. Flaxen suckers wiggled on either side of the opening with such an explicit invitation.

It only took one glance at his perfect body to stir Harrison's cock to life.

Whatever Lazlo wanted to do to him, he'd allow it. No. That wasn't quite accurate.

He *needed* to be fucked by him as thoroughly as possible. In that fiery hot moment, Harrison was convinced the only way he'd be able to prove his love was to be completely consumed by the pleasure demon and his tentacles.

"Come here." Lazlo waved Harrison over with a single finger. "Finish what you started earlier."

Gladly.

Harrison tossed his things on the bed as he closed the gap between him and Lazlo. When his arms wrapped around Lazlo's shoulders, the tentacles were quick to twine around Harrison's limbs and hips. They were warmer than before— perhaps because of the way they glowed—and being in their grasp once more was heavenly.

But more divine than being held by Lazlo was kissing him. The demon's mouth was so hot and sweet. With no need to rush, Harrison allowed his tongue to explore the gems inside his partner's mouth. When he brushed against the suckers under Lazlo's tongue, they pulled him closer.

As their lips settled into a comfortable rhythm, Harrison began to explore more of Lazlo's body with his hands. Burying his fingers in the demon's silky tresses sent a shiver down his spine. Caressing the gems on Lazlo's soft skin caused the hairs on his own arms to stiffen.

For the first time in his life, Harrison tingled from head to toe.

The more he touched Lazlo, the harder it became to stand. Harrison had become so turned on by what they were doing—and the hope they would be doing a lot more very soon. Before that very minute, he didn't know his bones were capable of turning into jelly from wanting to suck something so damn bad.

As if Lazlo could read his thoughts, a tentacle began probing at his lips. Harrison greedily broke from their kiss and allowed the new appendage to fill the space where Lazlo's tongue had been. The urge to drop to his knees and let the tentacle fuck his mouth overwhelmed him. It didn't help that Lazlo had the audacity to cock a pleased grin as he teased Harrison's mouth.

God, he was so sexy.

"You're wearing way too many clothes right now, did you know that?" Lazlo traced his nails along Harrison's collarbone. "Let's fix that."

The appendages around Harrison let go of him, but the one in his mouth stayed. Carefully, Harrison attempted to undo his belt while sucking on the warm tentacle, but he couldn't multitask with his raging boner and the sheer excitement of everything.

Lazlo stepped back, taking all of his tentacles with him. A whine trailed out of Harrison as the emptiness hit him. Another whimper followed when the tentacles nudged him toward the bed, but this noise was tinted with eagerness.

Harrison fell backward on the bed and finally managed to get his belt and jeans off. The tentacles swatted his hands away.

"Let me," Lazlo muttered as he approached the bed. "I like that you're a little clumsy now when you're usually so smooth."

"Me? Smooth?" Harrison couldn't help laughing. "I wish."

The remnants of his amusement faded as Lazlo's tentacles began to strip him. With every item of clothing they discarded, the long appendages rubbed against the exposed flesh. Each touch sent a jolt of pleasure through Harrison's body. The individual jolts swiftly blurred into one massive wave of bliss as he became covered in curious tentacles.

He had never counted how many tentacles Lazlo had before. Right now, it felt there were at least a hundred on his body.

Once the appendages had fully liberated Harrison from his clothes, Lazlo climbed on top of him. A promise to change the human's life sparkled in his smirk as he hovered over Harrison's twitching cock.

Lazlo brought a nail to Harrison's nipple and lazily drew a circle around it. "I always suspected that adorable flush you get in your cheeks and neck would travel down the rest of you."

"Does it?" Harrison asked, acutely aware he was growing redder with the question. His whole body felt like an over-heated circular saw. And he wobbled just like the tool would.

Lazlo nodded, a little chuckle following his smile. "What should I do to you?"

"Everything."

Harrison ran his tongue along his lip, unable to look at anything except the sunset palette glowing from the demon. His chest was tight with anticipation—and a drop of fear. He had no idea what all Lazlo could do to him.

But he wanted to know. *Had* to find out. If it took a century to discover the depths of Lazlo's talents, so be it.

Harrison Hamilton was happily in love. Though Lazlo hadn't said it as well, he knew his affections were returned. Climbing into bed for kicks alone wasn't something the demon wanted to do anymore.

Gratefulness and need rolled through the human as the demon teased the tip of Harrison's cock with his dripping wet opening.

"Never need lube, do you?" Harrison muttered, wishing his lover would hurry up and sink all the way down.

"Neither will you."

To Harrison's delight, one of the thinner tentacles penetrated the demon's opening. A light moan filled the space between them as the demon pleasured himself. Watching him like this was both wonderful and frustrating for the horny human. Was there enough space for both Lazlo's tentacle and his cock in there?

Before Harrison could get too antsy, Lazlo's tentacle slipped out, now coated in a gossamer veil of his natural slickness. Two more tentacles wrapped around Harrison's waist, forcing him to arch his hips. It became immediately obvious what Lazlo's intentions were as the glossy tentacle slid along Harrison's ass.

"Don't worry. I'll be gentle."

The human had fucked himself with toys in the past, but there was still nothing that could have prepared him enough for the shocking sensation of a wet, wiggly limb teasing his anus. With every sucker Harrison felt at his most intimate area, his appreciative groans grew in frequency. Once the tentacle had stretched him out enough to get inside a few inches, the appendage hardened.

And it felt. So. Damn. Good.

The whole time, Lazlo watched with a playful curl of his lips and a seductive arch of his eyebrow.

Harrison moaned as the hard tentacle slid further in him. "Fuck, you know how good at this you are, don't you?"

Lazlo leaned forward and pressed a kiss to Harrison's forehead. He continued answering the question by dragging his lips down the side of his jaw, a soft contrast to what was happening below the waist.

Just as Harrison got used to having the tentacle inside him, another new sensation hit him. His entire shaft had become swallowed by Lazlo's entrance. The suckers clung to his base, inviting Harrison to stay inside the hot, slick, tight space for as long as he wanted.

Everything felt dizzyingly perfect in that moment. They were inside each other, unable to get any closer to becoming one creature. Harrison's body started shivering and twitching against his will. It was ready to fuck as hard as possible.

But as soon as he had decided this was the height of pleasure, Lazlo proved him wrong. The demon balanced himself with one arm as the rest of his tentacles laced around Harrison's body, and his smirk broadened when he made eye contact with the flustered human.

"We're only just starting, you know?" Lazlo lowered his head and brought his mouth to Harrison's collarbone.

"Really?" Harrison gasped. "I already think I'm going to explode inside you."

"Oh?"

The aura around Lazlo grew bigger. It was almost too bright to look at him directly. He shifted forward, causing Harrison to slip partially out of his entrance. The tentacle in Harrison's ass moved in rhythm with the demon's motion.

Lazlo nuzzled Harrison's neck and placed a few more gentle kisses along the skin. "Go ahead. Come when you need to. In me. I'll get you excited enough for another orgasm."

"Is that a promise?"

The tentacles holding him tightened as if to reassure him. With the appendages wrapped around his neck, his arms, his chest, and his thighs, Harrison couldn't move. Not that he had anywhere else he wanted to be. With Lazlo's nails teasing his nipples, the demon's soft mouth on his collarbone, and his entire lower body being played with, it was impossible to imagine doing anything else but this.

Why had it taken so long for the two to meet?

Lazlo lead the beat of their lovemaking, keeping the tempo slow and steady. Even his hums of pleasure followed the cadence. Harrison, on the other hand, was lost in the bliss and unable to control himself or the sounds out of his mouth. Every moment felt better than the last, which was excruciating for a human who didn't want to orgasm so soon. He had never had multiple orgasms in quick succession.

But if there was anyone who could get his body riled up again at the speed of lightning, it would be the warm, thick, tentacled demon on top of him.

"Kiss me," Harrison weakly pleaded, so dangerously close to shattering. "Please."

A light laugh danced in the air as Lazlo's lips met his. Once Harrison could feel the gems in the demon's mouth, he closed his eyes and surrendered fully to him. There was no way they could be any closer. He never thought he could be tangled up like this with anyone. Physically and emotionally.

The low, heavy, guttural groan from his lover as Harrison climaxed rang in his ears so sweetly, so perfectly.

Lazlo and Harrison stilled their movements. The human needed to catch his breath as he cooled down, and the demon...

Harrison opened his eyes and broke into a wide smile. Every inch of Lazlo, still anchored to his cock and tentacle-deep inside him, sparkled. Sweat dripped down his body like liquid gold.

"You've got to be the most gorgeous creature to ever exist." Harrison let out a sigh, enjoying the way the tentacles still held him.

"I was actually just thinking the same thing about you."

Lazlo grinned. The glow around him had yet to fade, which elicited a flutter of Harrison's heart. Though he couldn't explain for sure how he knew, he was quite aware that glow indicated Lazlo was nowhere done with him, even with the demon's slit full of his cum.

Though Harrison enjoyed being pinned to his bed like this, part of him wanted to run his fingers through Lazlo's hair and cover as much of him as he could in kisses. Just for a minute.

Harrison nodded to their lower bodies. "Do you get energy from this?"

"I do." Lazlo sat up straight and rubbed his stomach. His grin twisted into a teasing smirk. "I'm so full of energy now. It makes me want to fuck you more."

Those words were all the human needed to have the fire inside him grow to life again.

"Keep going, then." Harrison met Lazlo's gorgeous, focused eyes. His heart pounded against his ribcage as he uttered his desires. "Fuck me until you can't physically do it anymore. Get all the energy you need. I want you to have it. I want to do *everything* you want to do."

"Everything?" Lazlo murmured, leaning forward and bringing his hand to Harrison's jaw. "You're sure?"

A large tentacle teased the edge of Harrison's mouth. All the human could do was eke out the neediest yes as his body became desperate to find out how much of the demon it could take.

Lazlo covered his mouth over Harrison's quickly, then he sat back up again.

"Keep your eyes open." His command was concise, but firm. "Keep looking at me. The moment you look away, that's when I'll stop. Understand?"

"Y-Yes."

The tentacles binding Harrison tightened, including the one around his neck. Fear froze his brain for a moment, but it passed as he settled his gaze on his lover.

He trusted Lazlo. In ways he could never describe to anyone, he knew the demon would take care of him tonight.

And, hopefully, forever.

Eagerly, Harrison let the tentacle pass through his lips. The warm appendage hardened in his mouth.

"Good, good, good." Lazlo's voice had grown impossibly soft. Each note struck Harrison with just as much pleasure as the subtle shifts of their tangled lower bodies. "I'll make sure you fill me up so good that I won't need to bang anyone else for centuries. Not that that's going to stop me from getting this thick cock in me and your lovely mouth around my limbs every night."

A muffled moan escaped Harrison. When Lazlo began rocking again, Harrison was treated to being fucked in three different ways. The tentacles in his mouth and ass slid in and out of him with a gentle rhythm, and his dick grew to life inside Lazlo. So many suckers clung to him as they moved, as if to promise the pair would spend eternity in bed.

With such bliss overwhelming him, it was hard for the excited human to say if he ever wanted to do anything except have sex with his demon boyfriend.

Not that he could physically say anything right now with a tentacle testing his gag reflex.

Lazlo kept his movements on the slow and easy side. Once again, he was teasing Harrison. It was a most delightful torture, getting slowly fucked by two rigid tentacles and a slick hole.

Every time he wanted the actions to be sped up, though, the tentacle around his neck would squeeze him enough to steal his breath and remind him that the demon on top of him was in charge. There was no room for anything like oxygen when he was so full of Lazlo. Harrison hardly dared to blink, though, because he had to last as long as possible. Had to find out what all his lover would do.

While still fucking Harrison, Lazlo held up the pack of forgotten cigarettes beside them. "Mind if I smoke?"

Huh? Now?

But Harrison nodded, unable to deny him anything while his body was brimming with pleasure. With every thrust, the tentacle went a little deeper down his throat. He was so, so close to choking on it—which made him so fucking hard.

Lazlo brought a cigarette to his mouth. The second it touched him, the white tip glowed like the rest of him. His gaze never left Harrison's as he took a long, luxurious drag. It was mesmerizing to watch the cloud of smoke leave Lazlo's ruby red lips.

"How does it look when I do this?" Lazlo asked. "Is it as hot as when you do it?"

Responding was difficult while sucking off a large tentacle. And the demon had begun to rock with him harder, faster. All Harrison could think about was how he needed to keep looking at his sexy lover. The fire in him had to burn for as long as possible. Everything felt so, so amazing.

Lazlo leaned forward, still smoking. Harrison's hips bucked against his as their pace increased. The tentacles holding him tightened more, keeping him moored.

"Don't look away from me, babe." Lazlo kept riding him roughly, kept drowning Harrison in his incredibleness. "Let me see how much you love being with me."

The demon squeezed the human's neck more and leisurely blew smoke into his mouth, all with a knowing smirk.

*Goddamn.*

Harrison had never wanted to smoke so bad in life. Nor had he ever needed to come so hard.

"Do it." The aura around Lazlo and strangled moans filled the room. "Your face says it all. Come in me. Give me every drop of your love."

With his eyes locked on the demon who had captured his heart, Harrison enjoyed the most powerful orgasm of his life.

His dick was still hard as Lazlo climbed off him and all the tentacles left his body. The emptiness that hit was too sudden for his brain to fully process what had just happened.

And, truthfully, the flames of passion continued to consume him.

Lazlo rolled over and handed him the cigarette, which he quickly accepted. After a quick, deliriously sweet puff, Harrison put out the cigarette along his nightstand.

"You're going to ruin a nice piece of oak like that?" Lazlo chuckled. "I could have gotten an ashtray for you."

"No time."

Harrison climbed on top of Lazlo. Surprise crossed the demon's expression, but he didn't move away. Instead, he wrapped his arms around Harrison's neck as the human covered Lazlo in kisses.

"You need more, don't you?" Harrison guided his cock toward Lazlo's drenched, sticky slit. The wriggling suckers at his entrance brushed against Harrison's tip, inviting him to come in. "I told you I'd prove how much I love you. You've already shown me your love, haven't you?"

"I..." A groan rolled out of Lazlo. He buried his face in Harrison's neck. "Yes. I love you so much. Give me everything."

All thoughts cleared out of Harrison as his hormones surged through him. There was no gentleness to his movements. His body had a need to ensure Lazlo would never be left in doubt of the human's affections for him. He pounded the needy demon with everything he had, hardly caring if the bed frame put a hole in the wall.

Which it did.

After a few minutes of vigorous fucking, framed by Lazlo muttering his name over and over, the demon shuddered.

The suckers at Harrison's base tightened, and a squad of tentacles wrapped around his legs and waist. A third orgasm poured out of him by the sudden confinement.

As he came, Lazlo let out a loud, long moan. No better song had ever filled Harrison's ears.

Lazlo let go of Harrison after a quiet, still moment. The glow around the demon had disappeared by now. Harrison rolled next to Lazlo and cuddled close to him, peppering him with kisses.

"If you're going to treat me like *that*, I'm not ever going to leave." Lazlo whimpered. "I don't think I've ever been banged like that before."

"Good. I don't want you to leave." Harrison fumbled for the cigarette pack, but it had become lost in the crumpled, wet blankets. "Just stay here. We can get your things tomorrow. Hopefully you're okay with some hamster housemates."

Lazlo broke into a hearty chuckle. "You mean it, don't you? Ah. I guess that judgment demon knew what he was doing when he told me to dig through some trash."

"Looking for trash meant finding me, huh?"

"Don't you humans have a saying? 'One man's trash is another man's boyfriend?'"

Harrison pressed his lips together, unwilling to correct him. "You hungry? I have leftover donair pizza downstairs."

"Leftovers!" Lazlo jumped out of bed, the evidence of their lovemaking dripping down the tentacles closest to his slit. "That's one step away from garbage, you know."

All Harrison could do was smile.

# EPILOGUE

"*Y*ou're throwing *this* away, Hamtaro? Really?" Lazlo held up a discarded delivery package. "You can put it in the recycle bin after you remove the label."

"Can I?" Harrison pulled out his phone from his pocket. "Are you an expert in recycling too?"

"Well." Lazlo shrugged. His tentacles wiggled in sync with his shoulders. "To an extent. I'm mostly just into trash, you know?"

Harrison flashed him a cheesy smile as he leaned against the kitchen island. "And me."

"And you, birthday boy."

Harrison chuckled to himself. It was strange to believe that he was forty when he felt like a twenty-year-old around Lazlo.

The time on his phone indicated it was now five o'clock. Justin should have been there by now. The concerned dad sent a text to his son. *When are you arriving?*

It didn't take long to get a response.

*Buying some beers for us since its your bday. I'll be there in less than ten. Does Lazlo like anything in particular?*

*Cheap shit lol. Just like me.*

Harrison swiped to the food delivery app after sending his response.

Only a week had passed since the night that changed everything. Life had been chaotic between sorting things with Justin's shitty ex-bosses (who were quick to cough up the dough when threatened with litigation), multiple sites needing an expert windows installer, and his boyfriend moving into the house.

Lazlo had only brought a couple of items with him—his work badge and keys. The demon had spent the past few evenings repurposing Harrison's clothes that had been collecting dust in the back of the closet. While he cut holes in shirts, he would talk to the hamsters in some attempt to get them to like him.

Tiger and Leopard apparently perceived the real Lazlo, so the first few days had involved them hiding in their bedding. Today, they were more curious about him. Not enough to let him touch them, but maybe they would get there one day.

Lazlo claimed he had never had a need to put on a disguise for animals. Only humans posed a danger to him. Neither of them truly knew why Harrison had been able to see past the magic, though Harrison had hoped it was just meant to be that way.

A ribbon of regret tied itself around the human's heart as he perused the menu options. It was a shame that Justin would only see the handsome fake human instead of the real Lazlo. While Lazlo's warm, funny personality shined through his words alone, Harrison wasn't looking forward to hiding a very real part of his relationship. It didn't matter if Gary or any of the other Happy Handymen thought of Lazlo as a human, but Justin…

Perhaps there wasn't realistically a way for Harrison to have everything he wanted. To be fully honest with himself *and* the people who accepted him for he was.

But he had Lazlo. And Justin was going to love him. That would be enough.

"Justin'll be here soon," Harrison said. "Anything you want for food? I'm ordering now."

"Nah, you decide." Lazlo closed the lid of the trash can. "I'll go wash up."

The demon slithered away to the downstairs bathroom. After a silent debate with his stomach, Harrison decided to get a variety of appetizers and wings from a nearby barbecue place. Plenty of messy, greasy food to go with the beer. He added three cheesecake slices to the order so they could watch the hockey game during dessert.

It was going to be a great night. Though Harrison was a little nervous, he was mostly excited. There was no other way he wanted to celebrate his birthday than by having all the people (and hamsters) he loved under the same roof.

And hopefully Justin wouldn't wander into Harrison and Lazlo's bedroom. Quite a bit of damage had been done over the week that Harrison hadn't gotten around to repairing yet. He did *not* want to explain the hole in the ceiling.

As he heard the door unlock, Harrison rushed to the entryway. His son greeted him with a one-armed hug and handed him the pack of beer.

"Happy birthday, Dad!" Justin kicked off his shoes. "It must be a lucky week for both of us, because I got an A on all of my papers this week. I'm feeling good about my upcoming exams!"

"Excellent, but that's not luck that you got those A's. That's all *your* work." Harrison led him to the kitchen and set the beer in the fridge. "I just put in an order for barbecue and cheesecake. Do you want anything else? We should celebrate you too."

"No way. This is your day!" Justin glanced around and lowered his voice. "Where's Lazlo?"

"Washing up. He had been…"

Well, Harrison could explain the trash thing later. Maybe the three of them would get wasted and go explore the garbage in the alley behind the house. Fun little family bonding time.

Harrison pulled out a cold beer from the fridge. "Want a beverage now?"

"Sure!" Justin accepted the drink. "Is it okay if I stay the night, or did my new daddy move into my room?"

"You can stay." Harrison grinned. "There's always going to be space for you."

"Yeah? Not going to have a baby or set up a home gym?"

Harrison snorted, grabbing a couple of drinks for him and Lazlo. "Could you handle having a little sibling?"

"Nah. I like being the only kid and getting *all* the Christmas presents."

"Oh, hey! Justin's here! I've been dying to finally meet you!"

Lazlo's voice echoed through the house. Harrison held the drinks close to his tight chest. Okay, maybe he was more than a little nervous about his son meeting his boyfriend.

Everything about this dinner had to go right. Even if there was going to be a little lie. If the two didn't get along, he would be at a complete loss. Much in the same way he could never imagine life without Justin, he also couldn't picture himself without Lazlo at his side.

"Oh, hi!" Justin turned toward Lazlo as he entered the kitchen. "It's nice to m—"

Justin dropped his beer. Though he hadn't opened it, the can cracked, spewing amber beverage everywhere. It was

Harrison's honed instinct to reach for the paper towels, but one of Lazlo's tentacles grabbed the roll first.

Well, it wasn't out of character for his son to be messy. And they could all laugh about it later. Lazlo's good fake looks must have startled him.

"Don't worry," Lazlo cooed. "Looks like you got some on your jeans. You should go change. I'll get this cleaned up."

"Uh, yeah. I'll do that."

Justin turned back to Harrison, his eyes wider than hockey pucks. He gestured for his dad to follow him.

That...was strange. His grown kid certainly didn't need help changing his clothes.

An idea dawned on Harrison as he continued studying the bewilderedness etched in his son's face.

"You see the tentacles, don't you?" he asked.

Warmth flowed through his chest as hope filled him. Perhaps there didn't have to be any lies in their family, after all.

Justin clenched his teeth and nodded slowly.

*Yes!*

"Does he?" Lazlo picked up the broken beer can with a tentacle while the others diligently mopped up the mess. "Hey, that makes everything a lot easier!"

So much easier. Harrison could scarcely believe how wonderful forty was shaping up to be. No more lies. No more hiding any part of himself around the people who mattered.

Harrison flashed a wide smile and handed Justin another beer. "Drink up, buddy. Meet your new demon daddy."

# ABOUT THE AUTHOR

Chace Verity (they/them) is publishing queer as heck stories with a strong romantic focus, although queer friendships and found families are important too. Chace prefers to write fantasy but dabbles in contemporary and historical fiction as well. An American citizen & Canadian permanent resident, Chace will probably never be able to call a gallon of milk a "four-liter."

Subscribe to their newsletter for the latest updates!
https://chaceverity.substack.com/

# ALSO BY CHACE VERITY

**For fans of paranormal romance...**

*Deal with The Demon*

*The Demon Next Door*

**For fans of contemporary romance...**

*Team Phison*

*Team Phison Forever*

*The Blundering Billionaire*

*How to Be Good*

*The (Virtual) Bodyguard*

**For fans of fantasy romance...**

*My Heart Is Ready (The Absolutes #0.5)*

*Your Heart Will Grow (The Absolutes #1)*

*My Heart Is Yours (The Absolutes #1.5)*

*Your Heart Will Burn (The Absolutes #2)*

*Dithered Hearts (Dithered Hearts #1)*

*Illusive Wishes (Dithered Hearts #2)*

*The Masked Minotaur*

Made in the USA
Middletown, DE
15 January 2022

58790502R00073